MEET THE FORTUNES!

Fortune of the Month: Nolan Fortune
(aka Nolan Forte)

Age: 26

Vital Statistics: Six feet of tall, dark and
handsome—and he slays on the saxophone

Claim to Fame: "Nolan Forte" tours around
the country with a jazz band on weekends.
Nolan Fortune is a millionaire banker desperate
to keep a low profile.

Romantic Prospects: "Nolan Forte" swept
Lizzie Sullivan off her feet last Christmas. But
her feelings about Nolan Fortune are decidedly
more complicated.

"Those few weeks last December were some of
the best days of my life. I knew I'd never forget
Lizzie, but we were doomed from the start. How
was I supposed to tell her that my whole life was
a lie? Her beloved 'starving artist' is really...filthy
rich.

"I really believed a clean break was best. But
now I realize it was a terrible mistake. I—*we*—
have a daughter. I want to be there for her. I
want to be there for both of them. First, though,
I have to regain Lizzie's trust. She doesn't want
my money. She says she doesn't want me. I have
to make this Christmas count. Somehow, I have
to prove to Lizzie that, deep down, I'm the same
man she fell in love with..."

THE FORTUNES OF TEXAS

Dear Reader,

I'm so excited to be joining the Fortunes of Texas! I love this family and have had a lot of fun living among them. If you've read any of my other eighty-six Harlequin novels, you'll find typical ttq here, too. Things always take unexpected twists and turns on me and I learned a long time ago to quit trying to control them. This time a house showed up. Definitely not in my plan. But it was the plan Nolan and Lizzie came up with and this is their story, so their call!

I love Christmas time. I'm the Christmas-obsessed person with every single room in my house decorated—including wall art. It's switched out for the holiday season. I wear holiday clothes all season, too. I like the colors, the lights, the excitement—kind of like living with the Fortunes. But much more than that, I believe in the message of hope. Of the miracles that come through ordinary people. Of unconditional love that never dies. The Fortunes are hugely entertaining, the love is soul-deep real. I hope you'll find both in the following pages!

Merry Christmas from Nolan, Lizzie, baby Stella and me!

Tara Taylor Quinn

PS: I love to hear from my readers! You can find me on social media as Tara Taylor Quinn and at tarataylorquinn.com.

Fortune's Christmas Baby

Tara Taylor Quinn

Special thanks and acknowledgment to Tara Taylor Quinn for her contribution to the Fortunes of Texas continuity.

Recycling programs
for this product may
not exist in your area.

ISBN-13: 978-1-335-46619-8

Fortune's Christmas Baby

Copyright © 2018 by Harlequin Books S.A.

HARLEQUIN®
www.Harlequin.com

Printed in U.S.A.

Having written over eighty-five novels, **Tara Taylor Quinn** is a *USA TODAY* bestselling author with more than seven million copies sold. She is known for delivering intense, emotional fiction. Tara is a past president of Romance Writers of America and is a seven-time RWA RITA® Award finalist. She has also appeared on TV across the country, including *CBS Sunday Morning*. She supports the National Domestic Violence Hotline. If you need help, please contact 1-800-799-7233.

To my own precious Christmas Babies:
Morgan Marie, Baylor Raine and Finley Joseph.

You remind me that life is eternal
and love matters more than anything else.

Chapter One

He wanted to play.

Just not in Austin.

Weary from a year of major financial gains, youngest son banker in a family of bankers, Nolan Fortune, wanted—badly—to get out of his hometown of New Orleans.

He wanted to tune out the noise, close his eyes and sink deeply into the world where it was him and his saxophone. Making music, not money. Just for the couple weeks that the executives at Fortune Investments, himself included, were off work over the holidays.

He needed to pretend to be someone else. To wear jeans, a bit of stubble on his usually freshly shaven face and a black leather vest if he felt like it. The yearning inside of him had to have a chance to break free for a bit or he was going to get really cranky.

He wanted to be his other self—Nolan Forte.

He wanted to travel with the band he secretly gigged

with on weekends—the guys who had no idea he was a millionaire banker in a family of millionaire bankers—and get a little crazy. He wanted to be able to talk to people—women—and believe that he, not his money, was the main attraction.

A little crazy. Nothing harsh enough to land him in any kind of trouble. Or the news.

How spoiled was he that he was getting almost everything he wanted—the break, the time with the band, the stubble and jeans, the anonymity—and he still wasn't satisfied?

But Austin…damn.

"Sorry you were outvoted, man." Daly, their lead guitarist turned in the seat he was hogging to look at Nolan, who was stretched out in the seat behind him. The fifteen-passenger van had a lot of seats. The band had four guys.

"You planning to sulk the whole way there?" Daly came again.

He wasn't sulking. He was contemplating life.

His life.

"The Florida gig could have been good," he said halfheartedly. Not that anyone knew it, but he'd arranged the Florida offer himself, through a friend of a music shop owner he used to know.

"In a retirement resort? You're kidding, right?"

With a shrug, he sat up, dropping his feet to the floor. "I hear they have great light displays," he said, and then grinned. The answer was lame, even for him.

And the Austin gig, a repeat tour at a jazz club by the University of Texas from the year before, paid better than any gig the band had ever had. It made sense to go back.

"Hell, man, lightning might strike your sorry butt

twice," Daly continued, putting a wad of gum in his mouth, as he referred to Nolan's supposed success with the ladies the year before. Or rather, one lady in particular.

Good thing Daly didn't need his teeth to play, Nolan thought sourly. At the rate he chewed the sugary crap he was going to lose them all. In truth, Daly's gifted fingers on any stringed instrument he picked up were being sold way too short with their little part-time band. He belonged in Vegas or LA or New York. On a stage in the serious jazz clubs where the real music lovers went to listen—not just to party.

"What was her name?" Daly prompted. "Emily something?"

It was at least the tenth time the guy had brought up a subject Nolan was trying his best to forget.

Daly just wouldn't let it rest apparently. It wasn't like she was the only woman who'd tried to contact one, or all, of them through their website. After checking with Nolan, Branham, who managed the site for them, did what they always did when that happened. He blocked the address.

"Elizabeth," he said. "Her name was Elizabeth." And he shut his mouth, wishing he could shut down the slideshow in his brain as easily.

Elizabeth Sullivan.

Lizzie.

God, she'd been a beauty. Not in the usual Texas sense, with high hair and lots of makeup.

Not Lizzie. The first thing he'd noticed about her, besides her straight, long dark hair and natural look, was that she wasn't drinking. Not that first night. Or the second...

No. He was not going to indulge in another Elizabeth fest. He'd spent the past year getting her out of his system. Thanking his lucky stars that he'd gotten away before he'd done something stupid and ended up ruining his life like his big brother Austin had done.

Or falling in love, telling her who he really was and having her love his money more than she'd ever cared about him.

Nolan closed his eyes. They were still a good five hours out. Time enough to catch up on his sleep.

Because as soon as they got to town, he was hitting a bar. Any bar.

Not to play. They didn't go on until the next night. Friday to Friday for two weeks. Fourteen nights in a row, except for Christmas Eve and Christmas Day. But tonight he was going to drink. As much as he wanted. As late as he wanted. Whatever he wanted.

So there.

Yeah, that was the plan.

And it was good.

When the phone rang at five-thirty Friday morning, twenty-two-year-old Lizzie Sullivan did not want to answer. At all. During the second and third rings she considered closing her eyes right back up and getting what sleep she could. Stella had been up all night, every hour or two, it seemed, and would be wanting to eat again way too soon.

At three months old, the baby should be letting her get at least four hours' rest at a time. Sometimes she did.

Lizzie's breasts were sore from too many feedings in the last few hours. Her lower belly muscles—thanks to the emergency cesarean section that had saved her life—still were not right. And she did not want to get out of bed.

She answered on the fourth ring. She had to earn the money when she could, which was why she'd gone back to work just six weeks after giving birth. There'd be no more calls after that morning as the schools where she substitute taught—all she could get since she'd been due to give birth during the first month of the semester— would be on Christmas break for the next two weeks.

Alliant High School needed a sub for freshman English. Classes started in two hours. Telling the automated system "yes" when it asked if she could be there, Lizzie threw off her covers and stumbled for the bathroom.

She'd always hated getting out of bed, but was generally looking forward to the day by the time she was out of the shower. That day was no different. With the extra money, she could get Stella the set of talking books the baby had been fascinated with in the store the week before.

She had Ziploc bags in the freezer filled with pumped milk for Carmela to feed the baby today. Her roommate's last-year architecture classes were mostly at night to compensate for Lizzie's daytime work hours— and also because of her internship with the famous Keaton Fortune Whitfield. If Carmela had to leave, she'd take Stella to the grandma-age nanny the two of them had chosen together.

Thank God for Carmela Connors. Getting her as a college roommate had been the second best thing that had ever happened to her. Next in line only to Stella.

She was in her favorite chair in the living room, feeding Stella one last time right before she left, grateful to have the time to bond with her baby girl, when Carmela came in with two cups of tea and handed her one.

"It sucks that you have to work today," her amber-haired friend said, curling her long legs up under her on the couch and pulling a fleece blanket over her lap. "For you, that is. I'm glad, as always, to get to hang and play mommy with that little one."

Switching the baby to her other breast, Lizzie kissed the top of Stella's head and said, "I hate leaving her, but honestly, I'm glad they called. A chance to make some extra money is a good thing. Especially right before the holidays."

And time away from the baby was good, too. Instead of getting overwrought with the permanent and all-encompassing responsibility of being a single parent, she had time away…and then chafed to get home to her.

"Yeah, but wouldn't it be great to be independently wealthy? Even for just a day or two? Like, do you ever think about how it'd feel to win the lottery? Oh, no, wait, we'd have to play to do that."

Carmela's droll tone made her smile. But she shook her head, too. "I seriously don't want that kind of money."

Suddenly serious, Carmela gave her a warm look. "I know, sweetie. And I probably don't really want it, either."

Carmela was the only person in her current life who knew why Lizzie shuddered at the idea of being wealthy, the only one who knew how her life had changed when her parents had reconnected with a friend of her mother's from high school who'd married money. The Mahoneys had been great to them. Always inviting her parents to parties and dinners and charity functions that were way above their means, and paying for it all, too. Buying Lizzie lovely gifts for Christmas. Things her parents could never afford.

She'd been expected to feel grateful. Blessed. And

she'd tried so hard. But inside she'd struggled with having her parents gone so much. Somehow, when the Mahoneys had called, a trip out for ice cream was no longer important. The opportunities they offered were better than the three of them home laughing while they made chocolate chip cookies and her father gave himself a cookie dough mustache.

Maybe if the Mahoneys had had children, it would have been better. Or if Lizzie had had siblings. Maybe if they'd done things together as families, rather than Lizzie always being left behind. Maybe if her mom had seemed as peacefully happy as she'd been before Barbara Mahoney had moved home to Chicago. If she hadn't always constantly been making excuses for their home, or trying to get Lizzie to dress up more, do her hair nice, speak differently when the Mahoneys were around. And getting tense about her own hair, her own clothes. Like their real life embarrassed her.

"Don't you think, if your parents had lived, that they'd have eventually pulled away from those friends of theirs and returned to normal life?" Carmela's quiet question broke into her thoughts.

Rubbing Stella's cheek, silently promising her baby girl that she'd never lose sight of what mattered most, Lizzie glanced over at Carmela, flooded with a bout of happiness, of being right where she was meant to be. "I'm not sure," she said now. "I like to think so. I just know that the Mahoneys left nothing but money behind, while Mom and Dad had an asset that was priceless. And now I do, too." She looked at the baby, whose mouth had fallen away from her breast as she went to sleep, and then glanced back at Carmela. "It's so weird, you know," she continued as she righted her bra and shirt. "When I first found out I was pregnant and couldn't get ahold of Nolan, I was so scared and depressed, thinking my life was over. And now I see that everything happened just as it was meant to. We might have an odd little family here—me and her and you—and I might have some struggles ahead, being a single mom, but I love this baby more than I'd ever thought it possible to love anyone."

"And look at you. Even pregnant, you finished your degree and are now an officially certified music teacher," Carmela added, holding up her teacup in a mock salute.

"I have to be ready for the day you graduate and get that fabulous job offer," Lizzie told her friend.

They were a great family, the three of them. But they'd known from the beginning that it wouldn't last forever.

It was something she made a point to remember so that when the time came for change, she'd be ready and able to deal with it.

Yep. She was going to work. Christmas was coming. And Stella was healthy.

She had this.

Nolan made it to breakfast around noon. Jim Daly and Arnold Branham were off somewhere. Glenn Downing, their drummer, was already at a table when Nolan showed up at the diner next door to their small hotel not far from the club. He joined the fortysomething divorced father of two who never got his kids on Christmas.

They talked about music, as they always did. The four guys had met in a private jazz class when Nolan had been in college. Daly, Branham and Nolan had been students and Glenn their instructor. Glenn, a music scholar, had chosen life on the road over life in the classroom after obtaining his doctorate degree in music theory. He'd toured with various bands for two decades and now hired himself out on the local New Orleans scene and taught private classes. Daly was hoping to get with a full-time touring band. And Branham, the oldest of the three former jazz students, was still in college, taking a couple of classes a semester since he had to work full-time to afford tuition. He wanted to be a veterinarian. But he was damned good with wind instruments, too.

None of them knew Nolan's real story. And the email address he'd given them had been created specifically and only for them, as was the cell number for the phone he'd purchased when he'd first had the yen to take a jazz music class and had invented Nolan Forte. None of them had any idea he'd learned the sax from some of the greats while still in high school because his parents had been trying to keep him out of trouble. They knew he lived in New Orleans and had a business degree, but he'd told them he worked as a grunt at a desk job. Statistical analysis, which was close enough to banking that he could pull off a conversation, and boring enough that he never had to.

If he had his way—and he usually did—that's all they'd ever know.

Nolan spent his afternoon doing exactly what he'd told himself he would not do. He walked around familiar spots on campus, visited a coffee shop for a coffee he didn't want because he'd been there before, stopped in a restaurant just to look at a particular booth in the back corner and even made it by the apartment complex that had tried to steal his life away from him.

Well, the complex hadn't. The temptation within it had.

Lizzie.

Built into the side of a hill, the one-floor building stood almost a full story above the street.

Looking up at the window of her old apartment, picturing the bedroom beyond, he shook his head and moved on. He'd glorified the entire two-week episode, he was sure.

And he'd made the right choice, too, in breaking things off cold with Lizzie. And in coming back to Austin, too, as it turned out. He'd just wanted to take the walk down memory lane, to find the closure he needed to get her fully out of his system.

There was no way any relationship between them would have worked. She'd been having fun with a not-rich saxophone player. She'd made her views of a wealthy lifestyle quite clear, when she'd told him, after they made love for the first time, that it didn't matter to her that he was a struggling musician. Unlike most, she didn't yearn for financial abundance. In fact, she thought that money chained people, not set them free. The yearning inside him had agreed with her, even as warning bells had gone off.

The rest of him, the parts Lizzie didn't know at all, liked his Ferrari, his home, his ability to take two weeks off worry-free and pretend to be someone else. He loved his family—even when he didn't like them sometimes. He needed to be a solid, contributing part of the energetic Fortune clan.

He liked eating at the finest restaurants. Having the best seats at the theater. And having a driver at his disposal any time he wanted.

He particularly liked being able to fly off to Greece for a long weekend.

Problem was, he'd liked Lizzie, too. More than any woman he'd ever been with.

He'd liked her too much to challenge the feelings with reality. Better to love and leave, as they'd both planned, than introduce her to his life of wealth and have the money come between them. They were from different worlds and he'd already tried that route with a woman he'd met in college. It had been a disaster all the way around, and they'd both been hurt. Badly. One of Molly's brothers had tried to cash in on knowing him, by using the Fortune name, and Molly had expected Nolan to let it go, because they were all "family."

He'd let it go because it hadn't hurt his family, but he'd also had to let her go.

Whatever love he'd had for her had turned to resentment. And worse. He hadn't been willing to chance having the same thing happen to him and Lizzie when reality set in.

He'd never thought she'd have used his wealth in that way, but their enormous differences would have torn their love apart. And then there was the fact that he'd been duplicitous with her, even after sleeping with her. A lack of trust was definitely pavement on the road to resentment.

Taking the long way back to the cheesy hotel, Nolan played the whole Lizzie thing in his mind one more time. He checked himself, his choices, and knew he'd done the right thing, cutting himself off from her.

His oldest brother, Austin, Nolan's mentor from birth, had been down the Lizzie road, too, falling hard for a woman in just two weeks. It had turned into the biggest mistake of his life and it *had* hurt the family. Austin had been twenty-five when he'd married on the spot, the age Nolan had been when he'd met Lizzie.

Lizzie had been young, too, just like Kelly, Austin's ex. Twenty-one actually, the same age Kelly had been when she'd hoodwinked Austin.

Added to all that was Nolan's own habit for getting into mischief. He could see now that it had been a result of him yearning to break free that had sent him down the wrong roads. He'd dealt with that shadowy side his entire life. And paid for it, too.

Like the time he'd thought it would be cool to dare a couple of his sisters, Savannah and Belle, the younger ones, to jump off a cliff into a swimming hole twenty feet below. After he'd already taken the fall himself. Of course, since he'd dared them and was older than them, they'd done it. Though they were both successful, Savannah got sick, with a cold that then went into a bronchial infection, and had to miss the first two weeks of school.

Miles Fortune had been all up for grounding his son for the entire school year. One of his older brothers had talked him down to Nolan being Savannah's servant for the next month, in charge of collecting and delivering all her school assignments, too.

And then there'd been the time he'd climbed out his window to meet up with the teenage daughter of one of the ladies who'd cleaned their ten-thousand-square-foot mansion. Austin had covered for him then. Miles had never found out about that one.

But he was an adult now. His brother couldn't cover for him anymore.

He'd understood what he had to do. And he'd done it. Cut things off at the quick with Lizzie before they went too far. He'd thrown away her number. He'd changed his own. And he'd checked the band's website to make certain that there was nothing there that could possibly tie Nolan Forte to Nolan Fortune.

And then, like Austin, he'd concentrated on work.

When he and Lizzie had made love, they'd agreed that there'd be no promises. They'd just met and he was only in town a couple of weeks. And while they'd left open the possibility of being in touch after Nolan Forte's gig was up and he had to leave with the band, they'd never promised to be.

Back at the hotel that Friday afternoon a year later to the day he'd first met Lizzie, Nolan showered, pulled on black jeans and rolled up the sleeves of his white cotton shirt, leaving the top buttons undone. He put on a black leather vest with silver studs, stepped into his black leather cowboy boots and grabbed his sax.

Lizzie was the past.

He was ready to move into his future.

Chapter Two

"He's in town."

Carmela didn't say who. But Lizzie knew immediately who her best friend was talking about.

Sitting with Carmela at the used but good-quality wood kitchen table they'd found at an estate sale, Lizzie flitted through the lettuce and veggies in her bowl with her fork. She'd been home from school for an hour, had fed Stella, who was sleeping, and really just wanted to take a nap herself.

If not for the fact that it had been her turn to make dinner, she'd have taken a nap rather than grilling chicken and cutting veggies for the salads they were now eating.

"Hon?" Carmela put fingers on top of Lizzie's hand.

Lizzie stilled, but didn't look up. Or over at the baby sleeping in her swing, either. "I heard you."

She was trying not to let the knowledge seep in. She

didn't want to know. And most certainly didn't want to care.

She'd told herself—and Carmela, too, three months before—that she wasn't going anywhere near the jazz club over the holidays. If he was there, he was there. The fact had nothing to do with her.

Not anymore.

So why was her heart pounding in her chest, making it impossible for her to swallow even if she'd managed to get lettuce to her mouth and chew?

"You need to go see him."

That got her attention. And gave her strength, too. Head shooting upward, she gave her roommate an authoritative stare. "Absolutely not."

"He has a right to know."

Putting her bare foot up on her chair, she hugged her knee with both arms. "No."

Carmela didn't speak, but Lizzie could feel the other woman's striking gray stare burning into her, escalating the confusion roaring inside her.

Because as certain as she was that she was not going to see Nolan Forte ever again—in that lifetime or any other as far as she was concerned—she was equally aware that in some universe he had a right to know that he was a father.

Worse, and much more angst-producing, was the fact that Stella had a right for him to know. In case, someday, he wanted to know her.

Or had family that did.

Like her, he'd apparently had no family close enough with whom to spend the holidays the previous year. Aunt Betty, her only living relative, had been on a cruise with Wayne, Betty's companion of thirty years. Nolan hadn't mentioned anyone, nor said why he hadn't been with them.

She hadn't asked.

There hadn't been time. Or it had seemed that way. With less than two weeks to spend with him, she'd been far more interested in their shared interests, in just "them," than she'd been in any peripheral details.

When she'd found out they had a very real repercussion from their time together, she regretted that she knew almost nothing about him.

Funny, when they'd been together she'd felt like she knew him as well as she knew herself. Felt like they'd been connected before birth, destined to find each other.

Instead, she'd found herself pregnant by a ghost.

One who'd disconnected the number he'd given her. Or had given her a false number to begin with, which was more likely.

One who'd never used the number she'd given him. Not once. Ever.

"He made it very clear that he didn't want to hear anything I might have to say to him ever again," she dropped into the tense silence that had fallen between her and Carmela.

Her roommate wasn't eating, either, or sipping from the wine she'd poured. Carmela was worried about her. She got that.

Truth be known, there were days when she was kind of worried about herself. But it had been a rough few months, having her blood pressure shoot so high the day she'd gone into labor that she'd had a seizure, prompting an immediate cesarean section. Trying to take care of her baby on her own as much as she could afterward, worrying when her blood pressure kept spiking and when Stella failed to gain weight. She'd wondered, a time or two, in the dark of the night, if they were both going to die.

They hadn't. She'd completely recovered from the pregnancy and postpartum-induced blood pressure issues. And Stella was a picture of perfect baby health.

But now Nolan was back in town.

The truth bobbed around in the outskirts of her awareness, as though testing her for reaction. She wasn't going to react, plain and simple.

"There is no way in hell I'm going back to that club," she said now. Despite that declaration, she couldn't help wondering how long he'd been in Austin, in her neighborhood.

He hadn't bothered to call. Or stop by.

It wasn't like he'd have forgotten where she lived. Unless he was a moron as well as a jackass.

He'd known she was a virgin. He'd made a big deal about how much it meant to him that he was her first time. Had made her feel so special. Cherished.

And then...he'd discarded her like she meant nothing at all.

Not even enough to deserve a real phone number. Or name.

She and Carmela had both spent months, on and off, searching the internet for any information on Nolan Forte. All roads led back to one place. His band's website.

At Carmela's urging, Lizzie had sent messages to the email listed on the site, with no reply.

"If he'd wanted his kid to have his name, he should have given the real one to her mother."

"I'm not suggesting that you try to hook up with him, hon." Carmela's tone was soft. "Just that this might be the only time you have a chance to tell him about

Stella." She rubbed Lizzie's arm. "I'm not championing him here," she said. "You know what I think of him."

In the very beginning, when Lizzie had first started seeing Nolan, Carmela had warned her against hanging out with a band member. Her boss's wife, Francesca Whitfield, had been in a relationship with a traveling band member for years—a boy she'd loved since high school—and had caught him cheating on her with a groupie.

Lizzie had thought Nolan was different.

"It's not because I give a rat's ass about him," Carmela started in again. "But you never know what the future's going to hold, sweetie. What if Stella needs him for some medical reason? A kidney match or something? You might need him to save her life and you'd have no way to find him. Or maybe he has family, a mother even, who'd love Stella, and you, too, for that matter? Chances are if she exists, she has a pretty good idea what a creep her son turned out to be."

She didn't need Nolan's mother to love her. Or anyone associated with him, either. She had Aunt Betty. And Carmela.

And the miracle of Stella.

If anyone had told her how her life would change the instant she held her baby in her arms, she'd never have believed them.

The way that baby filled her heart…made her feel strong and capable…and willing to give up her life at the same time, if it would save Stella's… It was transforming.

"You might be able to get support out of him," Carmela said.

"I don't want his money." She didn't want anything more from Nolan Forte. He'd given her enough. "And

I don't want him anywhere near Stella. He's a liar. A fake. If he'd pull a stunt like he did on me, pretending to be someone he wasn't, giving me an unusable phone number, who knows what he'd do if she was bugging him? Children believe everything they hear. And they expect their parents to be truthful to them. They don't need a parent they can't trust, one who will be constantly disappointing them. Besides, who knows, the guy might be a total creep. Could be the universe was watching out for me, keeping me safe, when it worked out like it did."

She'd had a lot of months to get herself right with the situation.

"Stella's going to need to know who he is someday. She's going to have a mind of her own and she'll need to know who fathered her."

"I'll tell her what I know. It'll be enough."

"You don't know that."

No. She didn't. The pang of guilt that hit her was unwelcome. As unwanted in her life as she was in Nolan Forte's.

He was in town and hadn't bothered to look her up.

"We're just going to have to cross that bridge when we come to it," she said now, standing to clear her plate from the table.

It had been a great night. Two long sets played to a completely full club. Setting his sax down on the stand where he'd leave it long enough to have a beer before packing up for the night, Nolan jumped down from the two-foot-high stage. Glenn would leave his drums set up. The mics would stay. Daly and Branham were already downing a couple of shots of whiskey and talking up the women who'd been flirting with them all night.

An older version of the two women at the bar with his bandmates stood to the side of the stage, talking to Glenn. The way she was smiling, leaning into him, touching his arm, she was doing more than asking about the band's schedule.

A woman who'd caught Nolan's eye a couple of times that night—only because he'd been looking over the crowd and she'd been staring at him each time—was lingering not far from the stage. After a couple of years on the road, he knew the probability existed that she was waiting for a chance to talk to him, maybe hang out for a while. And while Nolan Forte wasn't averse to little weekend flirtations now and then, just plain Nolan needed escape more.

And maybe a trip back to the hotel. He'd had a couple more beers than he should have had last night. Hitting the sack sounded not half-bad.

Now that he'd taken his walk down memory lane and gotten his closure, revisited his decisions and determined they'd been the right ones, concluding he was fully over Lizzie, he'd be out like a log. He'd probably have the best night's sleep he'd had in…well…a year, maybe.

"Hey."

The voice called out to him from behind just before he reached a corner of the bar. Swinging around, he felt his throat catch just when he'd begun to breathe easily for the first time all night. The sets were done and there'd been no Lizzie sighting.

He hadn't expected her to be there. But there'd been a small part of him that had insisted on hanging on to a minute bit of lingering doubt…

"Carmela, Lizzie's roommate," the woman said by way of introduction. "Remember me?"

"I didn't see you out there." He said the first thing that came to mind. And he forgave himself for not playing it cooler than that, considering the shock he was in seeing Lizzie's friend—someone who probably knew how she was.

"I timed my arrival for the ending of the last set. I couldn't be sure you wouldn't see me and bolt." The last was said with obvious derision.

He wasn't really getting her attitude. "I don't bolt."

"No, you just disappear."

"Look, I don't know what Lizzie told you, but we clearly said no strings attached. Her idea. She had very definite plans for her life and a struggling musician from out of town didn't fit them. We knew going in that it was only for two weeks. I was here for a gig, left when it was over. End of story." No one, not even Lizzie, knew of his inane and very dangerous struggle with his own wayward inner yearnings ever since.

"Not that I didn't enjoy my time with her," he was pushed to add. "I did. Very much. She's special."

"You gave her a bogus number."

The woman wouldn't quit.

"No, I didn't," he said, and then added, "I had to change carriers, and the number didn't convert."

True, to a point. He'd changed carriers for Nolan Forte's private phone, which had been the number he'd given her because he couldn't trust himself not to engage if she called.

"You never called her."

"Again, no expectation that I'd do so. We exchanged numbers, but made no promises either way. Her idea as much as mine."

He turned back to pick up his horn and get on out

of there. He'd pick up some comfort food on the way, take it back to his room.

Or he'd break his cardinal rule while on the road with the band and order a delivery that Nolan Fortune could easily afford. A thousand times over.

"You need to go see her."

Carmela's words at his back were a direct hit. She'd changed her tactics. Or he'd misheard the pleading in her tone now. He turned and looked at her.

"She's still in Austin?" He'd promised himself that wouldn't be the case, that she'd be graduated from college there and long gone. He only had two weeks to unwind, to recuperate from a long, hard, successful year of business. He needed the break. Deserved the break.

What he didn't need was drama from someone he hardly knew. His sisters provided plenty of that back in his real life.

Carmela stood there staring at him like she had a whole lot more to say. He commanded himself not to ask about Lizzie, but didn't obey.

"Didn't she graduate?" He'd have bet his entire fortune that she had.

"Yeah."

He shook his head, confused. "She got a job here in Austin, then? I was under the impression she planned to settle outside of Texas."

"She got a job, yeah," Carmela said, staring at him like he was supposed to be getting something more from what she was saying. He wasn't getting it.

"You two still roommates?" he asked to give himself time to figure out this uncomfortable encounter.

Surely Carmela didn't think he owed her something because he'd had a fling with her roommate.

"Yeah, we're still roommates," the fiery-haired woman said. "I don't graduate until spring."

So...wait a minute... "You're still in the same apartment?"

He'd been staring up at Lizzie's actual bedroom window that afternoon? He'd been a few feet away from her door? Walking around where he could have been discovered at any moment?

"Yeah," Carmela said, and then dropped her gaze. She glanced around the club, almost guilty-like. "You really need to go see her."

He couldn't. Not for anything. Just...no. He wasn't going back there again. He'd made it out.

He backed away from the woman.

"I'm serious, Nolan." Carmela took a step forward.

"If she wants to see me so badly why isn't she here?"

"I didn't say she wanted to see you."

Wait. What?

He shook his head. "Then why would I go see her?"

Once again her eyes met his, her stare like a slap. "I told Lizzie you were nothing special. That you were like all the rest, just out for a good time. She thought you were different. She thought you actually cared."

"We had a two-week thing."

"You messed her up, Forte," Carmela said, turning her back on him now. "If you have any decency in you at all, you need to go see her."

The woman's parting had him right back in hell, longing for what he couldn't have.

Chapter Three

When Carmela asked if she could take Stella with her to run errands Saturday morning, Lizzie didn't think twice. Her friend had taken ownership of the baby like a second parent, was as fiercely protective as any parent would be and was happier just having Stella around. She also knew that sometimes Lizzie needed a little alone time at home.

Time to clean her bathroom, in preparation for maybe taking a bubble bath afterward. Time to pay bills, or answer emails, without having an ear to the monitor and a fifty-fifty chance of being interrupted.

Time to answer the door when the bell rang just fifteen minutes after Carmela had left. She only had an hour or so, was in sweats and the T-shirt she'd pulled on to clean, and wasn't happy about the interruption.

Scouring pad in hand, blowing upward to move the stray hairs that had fallen from the clip holding up the knot on the top of her head, she looked through the peephole. And froze.

Tremors struck the hand that had automatically reached for the knob. Nolan was staring right at her and she had to remind herself that he couldn't see her.

But, oh, God, she could see him. That thick dark brown hair that had a tendency to curl just a bit, the jaw that really did jut with strength, the little bit of stubble. If she closed her eyes, which she was doing, she could still feel the rasp of his face against her skin.

Her lids shot open. He was still there. In black jeans and a red plaid button-down shirt visible through the open front of his leather jacket.

Her knees felt like she should sit down. The rest of her hummed with a peculiar energy she'd only ever felt once before in her life. For two weeks the year before.

The warm look in his dark brown gaze made her feel like he was focused right on her. Made her wish he was.

No.

She turned away. There was no law that said she had to open her door just because someone rang the bell. No way for him to know she was in there.

Carmela had taken her car. It had been easier than moving the car seat.

Car seat!

Nolan knew where she lived.

He was in town for two weeks.

Chances were if he wanted to see her—and he must since he was outside her door—then he'd come back if she didn't answer.

And when he did come back, chances were also good that if he found Lizzie home, Stella would be there, too.

She had to get rid of him now.

* * *

Nolan stood outside Lizzie's door, wanting this over and done with. Standing outside the door of his greatest temptation was not how he'd envisioned spending his Saturday morning. Carmela had said that she'd make sure Lizzie was home. And that she would not be. She was giving them time alone.

Why, he had no idea.

You messed her up, Forte. Carmela's words the night before had been haunting him ever since.

Open the damn door, Lizzie. Let me see what I did. So he could fix it and move on.

He was over her. He knew that much.

But he had spent the night trying to envision the damage he might have done. He'd never meant to hurt her. The whole point of leaving it like it had ended was so that neither of them would get hurt. Or resentful. It had been an incredible two weeks. A Christmas fantasy, as she'd once termed it. He'd wanted it to stay that way. For both of them. Instead, he'd messed her up?

How?

She'd graduated. Had a job. She wouldn't have gotten into drugs or alcohol. Not over a two-week romance. Not over him. The girl had survived the loss of her parents.

She was perfectly capable and comfortable with being alone in the world. Which was far more than he could ever see himself doing. The thought of not having his huge family in the background of his days was worse than any nightmare he'd ever had.

It was part of the reason he'd had to leave Lizzie behind. He couldn't be Nolan Forte full-time. His family needed Nolan Fortune. A capable, responsible Nolan Fortune, not a guy who was letting something unreliable inside of him drive actions that would point his life in an unsuccessful direction. Not a guy who'd repeat his own mistake by getting involved with someone completely outside their world.

His family wasn't the only entity that needed Nolan Fortune intact. He did, too. He was already less respected, being the baby boy of the family. He had to try harder, reach success faster, if he ever hoped to be an equal to his three older brothers.

He knocked a second time, hoping that maybe Carmela was wrong. Lizzie wasn't there. Or messed up, either.

A click sounded on the lock. The knob turned. As if in slow motion Nolan registered the door opening, not breathing as he waited to see her.

"Nolan. Wow. It's been a long time."

He backed up a couple of steps as the woman who'd been haunting him for an entire year slid outside, pulling the door closed but not latched behind herself, so that she could push back inside at any second.

She looked…divine. Perfect. His Lizzie, completely real, scouring pad and all. She did her own cleaning, twice a week, he remembered. He'd tried to help, but she'd kept shooing him away so mostly he'd watched. He'd gotten away with wiping the bathroom mirror. The sooner they'd got the bathroom clean, the sooner they'd be together in the garden-size tub…

He was hard. On fire. Having to consciously restrain himself from reaching out to her with both arms.

"Carmela said I messed you up." If he'd been anywhere near the vicinity of his right mind he'd never have spoken the words aloud.

The thought occurred to him that they could be in

on this together. *Messing* with him. For whatever un-
known reason.

The Lizzie he'd known would never have done that.
But then, that was the whole point, wasn't it? He'd only
known her for two weeks. The same amount of time
Austin had known his wife before he'd married her. And
Kelly had turned out to be a gold-digging, divorced,
in-debt daughter of jailed con artists, not the debutante
she'd presented to him.

He'd never have thought Molly would turn on him,
either, taking her brother's side.

"Carmela?" Lizzie's confused frown was damned
convincing.

"Your roommate? She is still your roommate, right?"
So far he was winning the battle with the hands in the
front pockets of his jeans. They were staying put.

"Yes. When did you speak to her?"

"Last night."

"You were here last night?" There was a slight squeak
to her voice as she looked around, and then back at him.
She was shivering.

It wasn't all that cold. Sixty or so. She had on a
T-shirt. The sun was shining. No need for him to offer
her his jacket.

"No, I wasn't here last night." Was he really doing
this? He had to get out of the craziness. He'd known
better.

"So how did you talk to her last night?" Even as she
asked, her eyes widened. "She went to the club." She
answered her own question.

He nodded.

The sudden stilling of everything about her, the
sharpening of her gaze, struck him as extremely non-

Lizzie. And that hint of fear he'd seen cross her expression? He had to have imagined that.

He might have had a fling with her and left, but he'd never, ever given her, or any other woman, any cause to fear him.

"What did she tell you?" The question was sharp, in a tone he'd never heard from her before.

"Nothing," he said, his frustration growing. "Just that I'd messed you up and needed to come see you."

The anger that flashed in her eyes wasn't hard at all to decipher, though the origin of it was not quite so clear. Either he or Carmela were in for it, though.

"She had no business going to see you."

Deciding the wisest course was to keep quiet until he could figure out what was going on, Nolan didn't voice his agreement on that one.

"And that's it?" she asked. "That's all she said?"

He nodded. He told himself she looked okay, so he could go. Should go.

Instead, he stayed glued to the spot.

"Well, as you can see, I'm fine. I'm sorry she bothered you. You can go now."

There. She confirmed it. Time to turn around and get back to his day. To walk aimlessly around the campus area and forget he'd ever known her.

Or see everything that reminded him of her and know that he'd made the right decision.

Maybe he should take a cab to the other side of the city and look at things he'd never seen before. Or, better yet, call home and get an update on all the drama he was missing. With six siblings, there always was some—a lot of times revolving around twenty-five-year-old Savannah. She was perhaps the smartest one of the bunch, but was way too beautiful for her own good, in

Nolan's opinion, and didn't take kindly to being told no, which he knew well. Having been born just a year before her, Nolan was the one who'd taken flak the most often when his sister didn't get her way.

"Please, Nolan, just go."

Lizzie's words, the honest pleading in them, brought him back fully to her doorstep. And the fact that he was still standing there.

"What did Carmela mean about you being messed up?" That's why he couldn't go. He was a gentleman and he had to know what was going on. To know his own culpability, or lack thereof, and take responsibility so that he could be completely free from what had turned out to be the most unfortunate incident in his life.

"I have no idea," Lizzie said. "I was…hurt…when you left and I couldn't get ahold of you. Maybe she wanted to give me a chance to chew you out. Maybe she thinks that would help. And, maybe for some, it would. I had no desire to hold on to any anger and I'm over it. Completely. As you can see, I'm fine."

Yes, she'd already said that. And she was guarding her door like a member of the Secret Service. It occurred to him then that she might have someone inside. A man would be the most obvious guess.

He turned to go. "Well, let her know I stopped by, will you? So she doesn't show up at the club again tonight ready to smash my grill."

She nodded. He took another step toward the parking lot and his escape. "You look good."

"I look like crap," she said. "I'm cleaning…" Her voice broke off, and she glanced away, almost as though she was also remembering the time he'd helped her clean the bathroom. That had been a Saturday morning, as well.

"So…Carmela said you graduated and got a job."

She nodded, and named the school district.

She had to really be all right, then, looking as great as she did and working for the city's public school system.

"Please, Nolan, I mean it. We had a great holiday. I really want to leave it at that. I'm asking you to leave now. And I'll talk to Carmela."

She looked so good.

"We could go for coffee. Just to catch up." What was he doing?

When she shook her head, he told himself he was relieved.

"Maybe later in the week, then. Come by the club, and we can set something up…just to talk…"

"Maybe. I need to get back inside." She took a small step back.

He had no more reason to stay then. Not a legitimate one. Wanting to give her a hug definitely wasn't one. Nor was he ready to just say goodbye. He was in town for a bit longer. They had a little time. With a last long look, he kept his hands in his pockets and headed back the way he'd come, wondering how long he'd wait for her to show up at the club before he'd break down and visit her again.

Chapter Four

After she slid back into her apartment, Lizzie bolted the door as though she could keep outside all of the feelings that seeing Nolan had brought back. Keep them in a pool out there. One she could avoid stepping into as she came and went from her home.

And after double-checking that the door was locked, she took her scouring pad back into her en-suite bathroom and sat on the side of the tub.

Just sat.

He'd looked so incredibly good. *So* good. So incredibly, bone-weakening, blood-heating good. If she was still alone and single, without responsibility, would she have asked him in?

Would she have regretted doing so?

What if he'd come when Stella had been home?

Oh. That was why Carmela had asked to take the baby on her errands that morning. Because it was something she did often enough that Lizzie wouldn't be curious. And it would also give Lizzie time alone with Nolan.

Her best friend and roommate hadn't told him about Stella.

She'd wanted Lizzie to do that. Had orchestrated the moment.

She'd overstepped. Lizzie was going to tell her so the second she got home.

In the meantime she recalled the warmth in that man's eyes. For a second there, it had been like the year before, like she could see clear to his soul. She'd never met a man who she felt such an instant connection to. Like she could trust him forever.

Ha.

The man who'd given her a bogus number. And obviously a fake name, too.

If she really wanted to know who he was she could go to the club. Get the skinny from any of his bandmates.

If she were really ballsy she could ask Nolan to see his driver's license.

Truth was, she no longer wanted the truth.

She wanted him gone.

He made it around the block. Twice. Two blocks over. Stopping for coffee Nolan sat himself down and looked around the shop at all of the people—mostly students and some professors who must live in the area, he presumed. A guy with glasses and longish, unkempt hair sat in a hoodie, hunched over a laptop that was plugged into the wall behind him.

A couple of girls leaned into each other across a table as they talked, one of them referring repeatedly to something on her phone.

He tried to imagine what it might be they were so engrossed in. A picture of a guy. A boyfriend. Maybe she'd caught him with another girl. Maybe they were looking at clothes. On their way to go shopping. Buying for themselves rather than picking up gifts for others.

Maybe he had to quit watching everyone else live their lives and live his own. He had to get back over to Lizzie's and tell her the truth about himself. He'd known, deep down, the second he'd seen her that he owed her that much.

Because of what they'd been to each other for the short holiday time.

He sat upright and noticed the clock up on the wall. He still had fifteen minutes, at the very least, before the hour was up that Carmela had assured him Lizzie would be home.

Alone. She'd said Lizzie would be home alone.

Which meant she hadn't had a guy in there, right?

He had to complete the unfinished business between them.

That was the answer.

His subterfuge, his lack of honesty, the way he'd changed his number—none of that was like him. It wasn't as decent as he needed to be.

That was the problem. Yeah, everything seemed to be coming clear now. Making total sense. It wasn't Lizzie compelling him; it was his own need to like himself. To be the man he thought himself to be. To live up to his own standards.

He'd never be fully free of her until he came clean. *I was...hurt...when you left and I couldn't get ahold of you...*

He felt again the stab her words had brought. Though he'd never meant to, he'd hurt her.

But that was in the past, he told himself.

But the truth wasn't. The truth was here and now. His to give.

He had to give her that.

Standing, feeling taller than he had in the past year, Nolan tossed his half-full cup into the trash and headed out the door.

She'd known he'd be back.

After all, she and Nolan had unfinished business. Like the baby he knew nothing about.

Leaving her unused scouring pad in the bathroom when she heard the bell, she went to the door, texting her roommate on the way.

He's here. Don't come back until I text the okay.

The rest, the part about her being unhappy with her friend's manipulation, however well-meaning, would be handled in person.

As before, she met him on the stoop outside her front door. She had some idea that they could walk down the short hill to the parking lot below. Anywhere but inside her apartment.

Her phone buzzed a text and she took a quick look.

Okay and good luck. Love you.

She wasn't telling him about Stella. Her mind was made up and Carmela's pressure couldn't change that. A decision like whether or not to tell the father of her baby that he had a child had to come from her.

"Look, I—I'm not planning to stalk you or anything," Nolan said, looking so...*Nolan* as he stood there on the small cement landing that served as their excuse for a porch. For a second there she could feel him again. Feel the warmth. The sense that, with him, she was complete.

Which was ludicrous. She'd known it back then, and she knew it now. They hardly knew each other. It had been the holidays and her being alone that had played with her head. Made her vulnerable to fall hard for the man who'd offered her a romantic fling in place of spending Christmas alone.

Carmela had offered to take her home to her family with her, but Lizzie hadn't wanted to go. Sometimes being a third wheel was worse than being alone.

Then she'd met Nolan. And had a two-week fairy tale. One she was remembering with too much intensity for her current well-being.

Her eyes lit on his mouth and her thoughts betrayed her as she felt an overwhelming desire to touch those lips with her own. But she was rational enough to know that kissing him would be the worst mistake she could make.

But to taste him one last time...

To be held in his arms...

No.

"I just... I needed to... Can we talk for a second?" he said when she got lost in her thoughts rather than responding. His hesitancy, so unlike the Nolan she'd known, had her curious.

"I kind of thought you'd be back," she told him. Maybe she shouldn't have. She didn't know. The *then* and *now* crashing into each other like they were was confusing her. "Neither one of us really got closure. So let's go ahead and get it and be done."

If only she could be certain her inner self would agree as readily as she wanted Nolan to do.

Watching her, he squinted, as though taking her mettle. When he nodded, she started to breathe a little easier.

"Can we go inside?"

"No!" She took a quick breath and tempered her response. "I don't think that's a good idea," she added more gently. "To be honest, I don't want you in my personal space. Whatever we have to say can be said right out here."

She glanced toward the parking lot, thinking maybe there'd be a car she didn't recognize out there, but didn't see one. The band traveled in a van. Last year he'd walked everywhere. Or she drove them.

"I'm sorry." He looked her in the eye when he offered the apology.

She believed he meant it. "Accepted," she said. And then, with an eye to getting rid of him for good this time, before she could be tempted to prolong the inevitable, she said, "Seriously, Nolan. I was upset when I tried to call you and the number was disconnected, but that was months ago. I'm really not harboring any hard feelings toward you, in spite of whatever Carmela might have insinuated."

"I lied to you."

She hadn't expected the outright admission but she said, "Okay."

"My real name isn't Nolan Forte."

Wow. The man was really unloading himself. Carmela must have done some number on him. When she was done chewing her roommate out for butting in someplace that wasn't her place to butt, she'd tell her how successful she'd been. Where Nolan was concerned only.

"But then, you already knew that, didn't you?"

If he was waiting for her to ask who he really was, he was going to be disappointed. She didn't want to care about that.

"Look, Nolan, or whoever you are, I've told you, it's fine. You're making much more of a big deal of this than necessary. I appreciate you stopping by. I don't feel as much like an inconsequential fling, and it's really fine. I moved on months ago."

He nodded, pivoted like he was about to leave and then turned back.

She would have liked to have been disappointed that it wasn't over yet. So why did she have that one-second shot of relief?

Because maybe she did need to know the truth?

To tell her daughter someday.

Or just to find that last bit of peace within herself. Who was this man who'd managed to get past her defenses, the carefully constructed walls and rules that kept her safe out in the big bad world all alone? How had he done so? And how could she be certain that it never happened again, with anyone else?

"The real me isn't someone you would like."

"I'm not all that fond of the you I know." Because he'd been a lie. But what was wrong with her? She didn't spit mean words at people, no matter how deserving. It just wasn't her way.

He acknowledged the hit with a bow of his head. It didn't make her feel good.

"Look, Nolan. It's not like you owed me anything. I just thought it was rude that you gave me a bogus number. The decent thing would have been to just let

it end. Not drag it out with the illusion of possibility."
She turned to go back in. This was done.

"When I left here I was open to the possibility."

Turning back, she stared at him. Her heart started to pound, constricting her breathing.

But it didn't matter. "Our entire time together was a lie, based on you being someone you weren't."

She'd known. But until he'd acknowledged that truth, there'd been hope that she was wrong. It wasn't until that moment that she realized she'd held on to that hope all these months in some small private recess of her heart.

"I *am* Nolan Forte," he said, still meeting her gaze head-on. "On as many weekends as I can manage and for two weeks over the Christmas holiday."

Confused, she reached behind her for the doorknob, not sure she was going in, but sure that she needed something to hold on to.

"Forte is my stage name."

She hadn't been important enough to be privy to anything other than that. So what did that make her, a common groupie? She felt stupid. She'd thought they were so much more than that.

He went on. "My family doesn't know."

About her? Or...

"They don't know you're Nolan Forte?"

He shook his head. "My oldest brother might suspect, but no, no one knows."

"You just disappear and they have no idea where you are?"

"Pretty much."

She had no idea what to do with that. So she focused elsewhere. He'd said "oldest brother." "How many brothers do you have?"

Her curiosity wasn't healthy. Still, she waited for his answer. Wondering *if* he'd answer.

"Three."

Wow. Four boys. For a second there, she was imagining a nice brick two-story somewhere with trampled grass and a basketball hoop hooked to the garage. Nolan was out there with his brothers, topping a couple of them, showing them how the game was played.

"I'm the youngest of the boys."

The imaginary video in her mind skidded to a halt and gave an instant replay. A little kid stood there now, watching the big guys play, wanting to play with them, but they wouldn't let him.

"I also have three sisters."

The mental video player disappeared. She stared at him. She'd thought they were both virtually alone in the world. Who, with a huge family, would be spending Christmas alone on the road, playing saxophone in a bar?

And then something else horrifying occurred to her. Maybe it should have before. Maybe in the darkest alleys in her mind it had.

"Are you married?"

"What?" His mouth dropped open and he frowned. "Are you kidding? Of course not! I wouldn't have..." He shook his head.

She felt like smiling. The sensation passed almost immediately.

He wasn't like her—mostly alone. Distance started to grow between her and the man she'd fallen so hard for the year before.

The man whose baby she'd had.

"My real name is Fortune." He said the words like they were a death sentence.

Feeling bereft at the loss she'd just suffered, finding out that they were not kindred spirits in the world of those with no family with whom to share the holidays, she shook her head. And then asked, "Is that your first name or your last name?"

"Last." His brow was still furrowed. She didn't much care. "You know my first name. It's Nolan."

So he'd only half lied on that one. She nodded, wishing that she'd never come out to talk to him a second time. Hoping to God that Carmela didn't betray her again and bring Stella back before she texted the okay.

Carmela... Her boss, the architect Keaton Fortune Whitfield... "Is your family into architecture?" It couldn't be. Stella was related to Carmela's boss?

"My family owns a financial investment firm in New Orleans. I work there."

She watched his mouth move. Wasn't sure she was taking in what he was saying.

"So you aren't related to Keaton Fortune Whitfield, the architect?" She suddenly wanted him to be the architect's cousin or something. Carmela liked and respected her boss.

Then she remembered... Keaton was an illegitimate son of a billionaire. It had been all over the news.

"No. We aren't part of the famous Fortune family, but we're probably as rich. My real life consists of everything you disdain," he continued. "While I own my own condo I still have my own suite of rooms in the family mansion. I love my luxury car, my hand-tailored suits and my ability to jump on a private plane and head to the Mediterranean for a long weekend. I love my family more than life and value my place among them as much. I take my responsibility to them seriously. As the youngest son, I am constantly having to prove myself. To earn respect. I work horridly long hours in the family business. I am very good at what I do, probably the best at it, but my life, my family, they consume me. And sometimes bore me."

As she listened to him, Lizzie's words from the year before came back to her, filling her with a completely new kind of tension.

You're exactly what I want to be...pursuing a career you love with passion, rather than being driven by wealth. I know not many would agree with me, but I feel sorry for insanely rich people. They're in a prison from which they'll never escape, being controlled by money. It exacts everything from you, but will leave you in an instant if you make a wrong move.

They were followed by a replay of his words of a moment ago.

My real life consists of everything you disdain.

There was no hope that he didn't remember her views on the wealthy.

Or that he shared them, either.

Sadness swamped her. Embarrassment. She'd been hanging out with a frickin' millionaire?

And anger was mixed in there, too. How dare he trick her like that! She went with the anger. It was easier.

"So...what...you were slumming for a couple of weeks, had your fun, and then when you realized that you'd given your number to a plebeian, you had it disconnected?" She'd brought him to her mundane little apartment with carpenter-grade doorknobs and linoleum on the floor.

The look of guilt that slid across his face was unmistakable, even as he said, "It wasn't like that, Lizzie. Not exactly. I never, ever for a second thought that I was slumming, or that you were any less than remarkable.

That time with you, it's right up there with the best experiences of my life."

The one thing he didn't deny was having his number disconnected.

He'd given it to her in the heat of the moment.

And when he'd returned home, he'd regretted having done so. Her heart gave its last little flop for him and went back in its box.

"Nolan Forte is a part of me," he said now. "I need him just like I need the other aspects of my life. He's what keeps me from going insane."

He couldn't be asking her to be around in the life of a guy who only existed on occasional weekends and a couple of weeks over Christmas, could he?

And was her heart actually feeling a resurgent flutter over that?

"Your family doesn't get together for Christmas?" she asked. And then reddened when she realized he could be Jewish, or some other faith that didn't celebrate even a secular form of the holiday.

"Oh, yeah, they do. It's total pandemonium."

"How do you get away with not being there?"

"Last year was the first time I even tried. The executive branch at the bank has vacation then, and I've always taken off for part of the time, and the fam lets me go my way without question, but I'm also always there for Christmas Day. Until last year. After I met you."

Oh.

"It didn't go over well," he told her.

After I met you. Meeting her had made him decide to diss his family?

"Even though you were playing in the band for the two-week gig, you still planned to go home for the day last year, and changed your mind when you found out

I was going to be here all alone." As truth dawned, the flood of confusing emotions was back.

"I couldn't lose what little time I had with you."

What little time he'd had. He'd known from the first moment he'd approached her in the bar the year before that there could never be anything between them except a secret moment in his life.

That might have been okay, if she'd known that, too.

He'd skipped his family Christmas to be with her. Which meant that the moment had meant something to him.

For a blip, that mattered.

And then it didn't.

Not when she recalled another word he'd uttered. It echoed in her mind. The *bank*? The "family business" was a *bank*? Good God, what had she inadvertently walked into? People with that much money had power. Lots of it.

He had power. She had Stella. Fear gripped her. Harder this time. She couldn't trust him. Nolan and his family, their wealth…could they take Stella from her? At least part-time? Break up her family? The Mahoneys had seemed to expect to get whatever they'd wanted, even when it came to disrupting Liz's family time. They hadn't seemed to have any sensitivity to her needs at all.

And they'd gotten exactly what they'd wanted, including her parents. Any time they'd asked.

Oh, God, she couldn't lose Stella, too.

"I appreciate you telling me the truth," she said, knowing that if she didn't end this soon, Carmela might get concerned and come back. Knowing, too, that she might not be thinking rationally. She needed time. And to be alone so she could think, when he wasn't distracting her. "I mean that. So…we have our closure. And now, I really do have things to do. I wish you the best, Nolan. I really do. And…thank you for…a two-week memory." She opened the door just enough to slip inside, locking it behind her.

She waited another fifteen minutes, long after she'd peeked out her bedroom window and seen Nolan Fortune walking away, to text her roommate to bring her baby home.

Chapter Five

Thirteen days. Minus Christmas, so twelve days. Twelve days. That was all he had to get through. He had the new arrangements to work on—scores written by Glenn specifically for the Austin gig. Sleep to catch up on.

Some reading to do.

He'd passed a couple of gyms between his apartment and Lizzie's place. He could get some workouts in. Hell, he could walk down to Rainey Street, check things out. He was a little old for party streets, and was working nights when things would really get going, but there'd be good eats among the historical homes turned bars.

What he couldn't seem to do that Saturday afternoon was get visions of Lizzie out of his mind. Or that…sense of her out of deeper parts of him. That sense…it was like she had some kind of power over him.

He couldn't have that.

Couldn't allow it. Or let himself get pulled under by it.

He'd just never have imagined how difficult it was to walk away from her.

Wealth came with privilege. And it came with detriment, too.

Which was why he had his two weeks away every year. And why he'd been so vulnerable to having the companionship of a woman who had no idea that he was rich.

Leaving the bar after an afternoon practice session on Saturday, he forced himself back to the hotel, rather than taking the walk back toward Lizzie's that his body was ordering him to take.

Just to see…

He'd been honest with her, confessing his lies, but telling her how much he'd cared, too.

He got that she didn't trust him. But if his leaving her with no way to contact him had bothered her that much, it meant she cared, too, right?

After his lies, he could see her being hesitant, perhaps wondering if he'd lied about other things with her, too. He could see her pulling back, but her sending him away…it wasn't sitting right. In the first place, if he didn't matter, if she was truly over "them," what would it hurt to chat? She'd been in such a hurry to get rid of him.

But it wasn't even her opposition to hanging out with him that was haunting him. What kept coming back to him, over and over throughout the day, was that odd look of fear that flashed in her eyes a time or two as they'd talked.

In all of his years, all of his relationships, Molly included, the one thing he'd never done was scare a woman. What on earth did she think she had to fear with him?

Carmela had said he'd messed her up. Lizzie had clearly been put out by him disconnecting the phone number he'd left her.

She'd had to have called it to know that.

Was it possible that she'd felt the same strong bond between them that his crazy self was telling him he'd felt? Did such a thing even exist outside the movies?

Had he broken her heart? Was that what she feared? Being hurt again?

Why had Carmela come to see him? What had she expected him to find?

Back at the hotel, his mind still reeled with questions. Almost to the point of obsession. He had to get her out of his system.

He had to know, to understand, what had really gone on between them, or not.

"So?" Carmela's question shot at Lizzie from the direction of the couch as she came from the bedroom she shared with Stella, having left the baby sleeping in her Pack 'n Play for the fifteen to forty-five minutes she'd stay there.

There'd been no time to talk earlier that day. The second Carmela had pulled up, Lizzie had taken the keys from Carmela and left. She'd run her own errands, going across town to get toothpaste and other incidentals so that she had no chance of running into Nolan Fortune. She'd thought about just keeping right on driving, into the next town, the next state.

"So, what?" she asked now, not even trying to hide her defensiveness. Carmela had stabbed her in the back, going behind her back as she had. She wanted to stay mad about that.

Anger was easier than the other debilitating emotions that had been threatening to suffocate her on and off all day. Not the least of which was a desire to see Nolan again. To find out what parts of him were real. To find out if he'd really cared.

"What did Nolan say when you told him about Stella?"

"I didn't tell him." And now came the really hard part. "You had no right to send him here, Carm. Or really to go see him at all. Not to talk about me. Stella is *my* daughter. The choices made on her behalf are mine to make. Period."

Every nerve in her body was shaking. She'd never talked to Carmela like that in her life and didn't want to be doing so now. In fact, she wouldn't have been if she didn't feel like a rat trapped in a corner, fighting for the right to breathe.

Expecting to see shock, and possibly hurt, on her best friend's face, telling herself she was ready for the fight, Lizzie was shocked when Carmela looked down at the architectural tome of a book she'd been reading, and said, "I know."

The beautiful amber-haired woman turned those gray eyes back on Lizzie with contrition, not the authoritative stare Lizzie had been expecting. "That's why I took her with me this morning," she said. "That and because just being with her makes me feel good. But…I worried all last night, and knew that I couldn't just let you open the door to him with Stella right there."

Lizzie sat down in the corner of the couch, turning toward her friend. "You could have told me this morning that you'd invited him over and let me decide whether or not to be here."

Carmela nodded, her brow furrowed. "I know. I thought about that, too. I just really thought, once you saw him, or he saw you, things would work out. I really thought that, deep down, you wanted to see him. Until you took Stella and left like that. I've been sick ever since. Please forgive me, Liz? It's just… I care so much…for both you and the baby. I see how much you're struggling—to pay bills, to find energy some days—and…it's not right. The guy might be a starving artist, but he should at least be helping you pay some of her expenses. How are you ever going to get ahead, or find happiness, if you're always running to catch up?"

Anger didn't have a chance with the love pouring out of Carmela. Truth was, it probably hadn't had a chance, anyway. She'd known that Carmela had only done what she did out of caring so much for her and Stella.

"I *am* happy, Carm," she said, speaking the truth that came from the very depths of her. "Stella gives me a joy I didn't even suspect existed. Yeah, I get tired, but I smile a lot, too."

"I know." Carmela smiled, and Lizzie grinned, as well, glad to have her friend back. Aunt Betty loved her. Lizzie and Stella would always have a home in Chicago in her old room in her aunt's apartment if she wanted to move back. But her aunt had a full life with someone else. Had a right to that life. Especially after being saddled with Lizzie without warning when her parents had been killed.

Ever since Lizzie had left for college, and met her freshman roommate, Carmela, she'd leaned on her aunt less. And Aunt Betty's life choices had included Lizzie less and less.

"Tell me what happened with him," Carmela said when Lizzie continued to just sit there.

"He told me the truth," she said, scared to death to say more. To make it more real. It was as if, once someone else knew, there'd be no going back.

What panicked her most was the fear that there was already no going back. Even if Nolan stayed away for the next thirteen days, or decided to ditch his holiday runaway hobby and hightail it home immediately, for fear that Carmela would spend the next two weeks hounding him, she could no longer be the woman she'd been before he'd knocked on her door.

Stella's father was tangible now.

It didn't change their day-to-day lives. She was praying that it didn't change anything for them. But she couldn't shake the fear.

"I know his real name. Where he's from," she said slowly as Carmela sat, completely silent for once. And then it occurred to her. "Did you already know? Did he tell you?"

"No." Carmela's head shake was definitive. "We didn't chat," she said now, her tone making clear that if there were sides to be drawn, Carmela and Nolan weren't on the same one. "I simply told him he needed to come see you and gave him a window of time in which you'd be home this morning." That last was said with a pleading look.

"He's ungodly rich, Carm. Like in, probably famous among moneyed people. I've never heard of him, but his family owns a frickin' investment bank!"

"What bank?"

"I don't know. He didn't say. I didn't ask. I haven't Googled him yet." She clamored around, looking for a way out. She didn't want to know which bank. Didn't want any of it to become more horrifyingly real.

Money meant power.

Which made her feel powerless.

While so many of her college friends were out partying on their parents' dime, Lizzie had been the student who'd had to work two jobs on campus, in addition to a fast food job, just to pay for incidentals and books. She was the one who'd be paying for the next ten years on all of the school loans she'd had to take out just to get through college.

Nolan's family owned a bank, while she owed a bank close to a hundred thousand dollars in student loans.

Not that she cared, personally. She and Nolan weren't a thing. But there was Stella…

Carmela seemed to ooze energy all of a sudden as she slid a little closer to Lizzie, leaning forward, her face alight as she said, "This is so great, Liz! DNA can prove paternity and you'll be home free!"

No! No. No. No.

She couldn't shake her head enough. Or stop the sudden tears that sprang to her eyes.

"He can't know about her," she whispered when Carmela stilled.

"He has to know about her, hon, he's her father."

She shook her head again, everything inside her crying out against the words Carmela had put into their living space.

"He's not named on her birth certificate. He wanted nothing more to do with me or the consequences of those two weeks last year. He deliberately disconnected the phone number he gave me, Carmela, leaving me no way to contact him. To include him in any decisions.

I did this. I made the choice to have her. He's an un-knowing sperm donor. That's all."

Carmela's silence was almost as painful as her words had been.

"He has a huge family." Lizzie said the words that had been giving her cold sweats since Nolan Fortune had announced his identity on her doorstep. "What if they want her? What if they sue for custody? I'd never have the money to fight them. They could take her away from me!"

"Aw, sweetie." Carmela scooted closer, took one of Lizzie's trembling hands and held on. "He can't take her away from you, even if he wanted to! You're her mother!"

She shook her head. "You don't know that," she said. "There's a different set of rules for rich people. Really rich people. Look at that kid in Texas who was driving drunk and killed those people and didn't even spend one day in jail because his family had power. It happens all the time. Read the news. Or just look at my past. The Mahoneys got what they wanted. They took my family, Carm. You don't know the insidious way money draws people to it, or makes them agree with those who have it. Besides, look around us. We give her a couple of rooms. Cheap floors. Box-store clothes. Public school is the only thing her future holds with me. They could probably give her the moon, if she wanted it. Or a trip to it at least."

Her last words hung there like a thick haze in the room. Lizzie had been hearing renditions of them in her mind all afternoon.

They always stopped right there. With that trip to the moon.

Just…

"And what about all that, hon?" Carmela's soft question came after minutes of silence. "Wouldn't you like your daughter to have those things? Doesn't Stella deserve the chance at every opportunity her father's family could give her?"

No! She meant to shake her head, but just started to shake instead.

"Money's not all it's cracked up to be." She said aloud the arguments she'd come up with to appease the other side of her fighting self. "A lot of rich kids grow up entitled. They have skewed senses of value. Of their own value. They miss out on a lot of important life lessons, like compassion for others, or an understanding of what it means to fend for yourself. Or the sense of satisfaction you get when you provide for yourself. They don't know the priceless value of sincere laughter. Or…or how a lifetime could be built in two weeks…"

Damn Nolan Fortune and his fake alter ego. He'd been out for a two-week escape. Had embarked on a holiday fling knowing it was no more than his little secret.

His little secret had created her little secret, and even if she wanted to tell him now…how could she? *Oh, by the way, I failed to mention earlier that I gave birth to your daughter a few months ago.*

He'd hate her.

And why should she care?

How could it possibly matter anymore what he thought of her? Yeah, believing that he'd cared as much as she had, that they were something different and deep and meaningful, was a nice fairy tale. And if, for a short time, she'd hoped that it could last, that hope was long dead.

The man was probably richer than the Mahoneys. There was no way she wanted him now.

"I want her to care more about the trials and joys of the majority of the people in society than she does about what designer brand she's going to wear to dinner," she finally answered.

"You're her mother. You'll teach her that."

"And you think, if she's growing up in their world, that she'll care what I have to teach her?" Lizzie had seen a fast-forwarded mental image of that, too. Her parents had been drawn to the Mahoneys' wealth and they'd been adults. How could she even hope that Stella, an innocent child, could remain immune? She could just see it, her own daughter eventually pitying her, looking down on her, the lowly public school teacher who'd gotten herself knocked up by someone she hardly knew during a holiday fling. Nothing in Lizzie's home would ever equal the grandeur and luxury that teenager would know in a mansion. Hell, they might give her some Mercedes sports car for her sixteenth birthday, and Stella wouldn't even be able to drive it to Lizzie's neighborhood without worrying about having it vandalized or stolen.

If she even wanted to be seen in such a plebeian neighborhood.

When the voices in her mind got too loud, she repeated much of it to Carmela, who listened, and then said, "You sound like a reverse snob," she said.

Yeah, maybe she did. But… "You can see it happening, though, can't you? There's a good chance."

"It's possible he won't want to have anything to do with her," Carmela said. "A good chance he'd just want to pay you off so that his family never found out about his trek to the common people—or his illegitimate child. You'd get to keep Stella all to yourself, *and* get financial freedom—enough to ensure that she gets whatever education she wants."

She'd thought of that. Was already certain that she wouldn't take a dime of Nolan's payoff money for herself. But if he wanted to set up a trust for Stella...

"I don't love the guy, Liz. As a matter of fact, I'm pretty sure I can't stand him. But he has a right to know that he fathered a child."

She was still debating that point. Would Nolan have wanted her to have the baby? Or would he have tried to force her to abort their fetus?

Carmella gave her hand a squeeze. "Stella's going to want to know who her father is, hon. And when you tell her, you know she's going to look him up. Want to contact him. Even if you tell her she can't, she'd more than likely do it behind your back. He's her father. A part of her."

Yeah, yeah, Lizzie'd been there, too, during her mental battles. Knowing her daughter would need more someday. And every time she thought about it, she ended up at another dead end.

Oh, God. What was she going to do?

With a throat that felt thick with tears, she said, "Have you ever heard of joint parenting between an überrich parent and a lower-middle-class parent working out?" she asked.

"Maybe in fairy tales," Carmela said, her tone mellow now, too, her expression sad.

"And that's when the princess is poor and secretly longs for a knight in shining armor to save her from the drudgery. But I'm not that. The thought of living a privileged life—having everyone paying attention to what you do, shining a light on any mistake you might make...having to do your hair every time you go out...having to live up to expectation, to keep up appearances, having to disguise yourself if you ever just want to feel regular, and doing things, accepting invitations, so as not to offend someone else important, not ever knowing that thrill you get when you earn enough money to buy something you really want—I'm not that."

Her list went on and on. Most of it she'd learned when her mother's high school friend returned to Chicago, but some were opinions she'd had strengthened through observations she'd made in life, too.

"I like being anonymous," she said. "It gives me the freedom to truly make my own choices based on what my heart tells me. To live authentically. That's what I want for Stella. To be able to truly follow her heart…not to have to live up to standards others set for her. That's the only way she'll be able to reach her true potential."

"So what's your heart telling you now?" Carmela's words put a stop to the thoughts clamoring in Lizzie's brain. Everything stilled. Almost. Everything but the fear.

Lizzie tried to listen to her heart. She'd been trying all day.

She took a deep breath and shuddered because…

"My heart tells me that I don't want Stella to grow up with only one or two people—me or you—to catch her if she falls," she said. "What if something happens to us?" She'd been an only child of a couple whose parents were all gone. "As you say, the Fortunes might not want her, but Nolan says he has a bunch of siblings. Stella has aunts and uncles. More than just one. She might have cousins. She has grandparents."

Stella had a big biological family.

Exactly what Lizzie had always wanted most.

And didn't have to give.

Chapter Six

Nolan gave every bit of energy he had to his sax, breathing his emotion into the instrument, telling himself that the music was all that mattered to him that night. He determined to be completely truthful to it, to let the notes evoke whatever part of him he had to give, to become one with the collaboration.

That's why he was there—in Austin, onstage at all—so that the hidden, secret parts of him could know expression to the fullest. To give positive outlet to the passion bottled up inside of him.

He blocked out the crowd, the drinkers and the women milling around. Normally his music was for them. Tonight he was playing for himself.

A brief release. That's all he needed. He'd give his full focus to others, be a top-notch contributor, the other fifty weeks of the year. He just needed a couple of weeks of unfiltered self-expression.

It was only between songs that he found himself scanning the audience for one specific brunette.

But she never turned up.

He'd really thought Lizzie would be in the club that night. Coming to him on her terms. Letting him know that she called the shots.

When the gig ended, he took his time about packing up. He stopped across the street from the club for a carton of chocolate milk to take back to the hotel with him.

He spent the night in a state of weird dream and restless wakefulness. At one point he got up and showered. A long hot cleansing. He let the water sluice over him, relaxing his muscles. Drying off, he wandered naked back to bed.

Half an hour later, he tried the television, flipping through channels, trying to find anything that would bore him to sleep.

When others were going to church Sunday morning, Nolan was wandering the streets in his jeans and black vest, arms bare except for the T-shirt he had on, oblivious to the fifty-degree chill. He'd wanted to be free of Lizzie's hold over him. He'd put the goal first and foremost on his list.

So that was what was happening. Maybe not the way he'd envisioned. Maybe not with him losing all the pent-up yearning for her, but with her rejecting him. Still, the end result was the same. He didn't have to worry anymore about his feelings for her controlling him and driving him to make poor choices that not only mucked up his life, but hurt his family, and her, too.

She wasn't willing to be party to any of his choices.

Seeing her there outside her door yesterday, with her looking at him as the man he was—Nolan Fortune, millionaire in his own right and joint heir to billions—had brought home to him the insane differences between them. It wasn't just about what block you lived on, or the size of your house or where you went to school. It was a way of life—hers, and then, in a completely different atmosphere, his.

Nolan Forte had been able to pretend he belonged in her apartment.

Nolan Fortune couldn't.

He still couldn't figure out why Carmela had come to find him. Insisted that Lizzie was messed up and needed to see him. She hadn't known about his alias so it couldn't have been his money she was after.

Lizzie hadn't appeared at all "messed up." In fact, she'd looked as incredible as he'd remembered. Better, really. She was curvier than a year ago, which he liked. A lot. He'd teased her before about being all skin and bones. She'd been on a tight budget and hadn't been eating enough, in his humble opinion.

But she'd had the same exact expression-filled brown eyes with insanely long lashes, beautiful skin and high cheekbones that set her apart, outlining that one-of-a-kind smile.

Not that he'd seen her smile yesterday. She hadn't been pleased to see him.

So maybe Lizzie had just needed closure—had needed the truth. Maybe Carmela had meant that he'd messed her up emotionally with his disappearing act. Given her an inability to trust. She'd obviously tried to call the number he'd given her, since she knew he'd had it disconnected. Maybe that had been playing with her—thinking that he'd deceived her about everything else, too.

He'd told some lies, but not about how much he'd enjoyed his time with her, or about how special she'd been.

He turned corners. Passed open coffee shops, a bagel place, a bakery. He heard church bells, avoided traffic.

And it dawned on him…he'd done it again. He'd left without giving Lizzie a way to contact him—other than the club for the next two weeks. He'd told her his name, but he'd still given her no access to Nolan Fortune. Maybe that's what she'd needed. Just to know that she hadn't been kicked aside.

Yeah, his pace picked up as he landed on the thought. Pulling out his phone, he was pretty sure he was on the right track. He'd call her, give her his real number, his private cell, not the one the band used. Tell her that if she ever needed anything, he'd like her to call him.

It's what a Fortune would do.

And one thing was unequivocally certain to Nolan these days. He was bound and determined—needed—to be a stand-up Fortune.

In spite of the emotions boiling inside of him.

Normally Lizzie was zonked from the second Stella fell back to sleep after her middle-of-the-night feeding until the baby woke up again just before dawn. It hadn't happened that way Saturday night and she was heading for a nap on the couch when Stella finally nodded off in her swing just after nine on Sunday morning. Carmela was at the library studying—she loved it there on Sunday mornings because it was so quiet—and while Lizzie had planned to get the Christmas decorations out and have the place festive and happy feeling by the time her roommate returned, she really just wanted to sleep.

In flannel pajama pants, her butt made it to the sofa cushion, but her head wasn't even on the pillow she'd punched into the arm of the couch when her cell rang.

Not recognizing the number, or even the area code,

that flashed on her screen, she let the call go to voice mail. Too many sales calls, debt consolidators and political robots these days. If the call was important, they could leave a voice message. She had to get some sleep.

Her eyes had just closed when she heard the faint ting of her voice-mail notification. She knew she wasn't going to be able to ignore it enough to doze off. She was going to lie there and wonder who'd left that message.

"Lizzie? This is Nolan Fortune. Listen, I'm not planning to harass you or anything. I just wanted to make sure you have my phone number this time. My personal cell number. Please call me if there's ever a time you need anything. I'll be happy to hear from you."

He'd be happy to hear from her?

Lying back down, her heart pounding and her belly flip-flopping, she tried to relax. He might be richer than Midas and he'd be happy to hear from a first-year schoolteacher who was living paycheck to paycheck?

That made no sense to her.

Panic flared as she considered the idea that he knew about Stella. That he was trying to worm his way in so that he and his big rich family could steal her baby away from her. Opening her eyes, she sat up.

The thought was ridiculous. If he knew about Stella, all he had to do was compel a warrant for her DNA. Hell, he didn't have to do it; he'd have any number of people under him who'd do it for him. Probably a team of high-powered lawyers.

Or maybe he was just looking for another romp over the holiday? Some men got turned on by women who weren't in their usual social circles. And she'd been a cheap date.

She'd just never *felt* cheap. Until she'd dialed the

number Nolan Forte had left her and found out that he'd been unreachable. In every fashion.

If he thought—

No. She'd seen him twice the day before. He'd seemed sincere both times.

Hadn't come on to her at all.

So did he know about Stella? Had he been spying on them?

No.

She wasn't going to lose her mind over this.

She was going to handle it.

She just had no idea how. No honest idea what was best for her daughter.

Because that was what it came down to. In conversations with Carmela. In the middle of the night. And midmorning, too. Her bottom line was Stella.

She'd do whatever was best for her daughter.

Even if that meant she lost the one thing that mattered more to her in the world. The one thing that had made her truly, completely happy. Being a family with her baby girl.

Nolan was that baby girl's father. Good or bad.

The day before, he'd seemed to really care that Lizzie was all right. He'd come clean with her when he'd had no reason to have to do so.

Maybe some aspects of the man she'd fallen so hard for were real. Maybe some of Nolan Forte really did exist in Nolan Fortune. Maybe she had to find out.

For Stella's sake, if nothing else.

Picking up her phone, she didn't add the last number to her contacts. She tried not to look at it long enough to remember it.

She called it.

And when he picked up on the first ring, she forced

words past the constriction in her chest, and hung up mere seconds later with an appointment to meet with Nolan for coffee that afternoon at a shop they'd frequented several times in the past.

Next she texted Carmela, making arrangements for her roommate to be home to tend to Stella while she was gone. Carmela, who was greatly relieved Lizzie had contacted Stella's father, agreed immediately, of course.

Lizzie had known she would.

And wished she hadn't.

Now she had no excuse to call back and cancel.

She had to sit across the table from the only man she'd ever loved and figure out if he was going to be the source of her greatest heartbreak.

For a second time.

Chapter Seven

Holy hell. He was sliding right back to the past, agreeing to spend Sunday afternoon sipping coffee with Lizzie. The hours that had to pass before then taunted him with anticipation versus responsibility. He walked, and then ran some, expending energy that continued to produce inside him at alarming rates.

Lizzie and him! Drinking coffee.

It couldn't be the past. And there was no future.

That thought firmly in mind, Nolan found a high-end clothing store open on Sunday, and while the gray suit, white shirt and blue silk tie he ended up with wasn't tailor-made to fit him, it was going to make him stand out among the college students, professors and general coffee-shop-goers by campus.

His jeans would have been more to his liking.

But he was a Fortune. He was going to feel like one. To act like one. To look like one.

He was not going to forget, even for a second, that Nolan Forte existed only in his deepest, unreliable yearnings. The man owned jeans, but he wasn't real.

He had to give Lizzie real.

Staring at the shiny toes of his brand-new black leather dress shoes, he waited for her outside the shop, his thumb rapping a beat against his thigh.

He had nothing to be nervous about.

She'd only wanted to talk.

He owed her that.

And then he'd walk away. It was the only choice he could live with.

In jeans and a purple loose-fitting T-shirt, Lizzie looked him right in the eye as she walked up to him. Her dark hair, down and straight, as usual, caught the sun's reflection and glinted like gold. Or the little white lights on a Christmas tree.

Giving himself a mental shake, he calmly held open the door for Lizzie to pass through before him. She gave no outward reaction to his changed appearance, and he had no reason to feel disappointed.

He was there to listen, not to get her attention.

Forte wanted to know what Lizzie thought of Fortune's looks. Just like a fantasy, to think about things that didn't matter.

She ordered tea, not the caramel latte she'd preferred the year before, and he allowed himself a small black coffee—laced with nothing—staying away from the espresso he'd have preferred. No surges of adrenaline or energy necessary at the moment. When he turned from paying at the counter, to notice the high-top table in the corner they'd shared several times the previous year, he'd expected her to head in that direction.

She chose instead an upholstered armchair, across

from another, with a square brown table in the center. Applauding her decision to put more distance between them than other tables would have done, he took the seat she'd left him, and sipped his coffee.

He tried not to notice that everything about her, from the backside he'd followed across the room, to the way she held her shoulders, matched perfectly the image he carried daily in his memory. He'd have preferred the real thing not to live up to fantasy.

What did a guy have to do to catch a break?

"So what's up?" He'd opened this door by giving her his number. And it felt wrong, too. Like he was breaking some kind of "good man" rule.

He had to be there, wanted to be there, and had nothing to offer that she'd want or need.

Her shrug didn't bode well for his quick finale. "I just…wanted to talk," she said slowly, as if just now figuring out a purpose for the meeting. "It plays with your head, you know, to think you had…something… and then find out that it wasn't real. I mean, I knew it wasn't permanent or anything. We made no commitments, but I really trusted you. I thought we were honestly special. Different from a usual hookup. When I first figured out that you'd been lying to me all along— you know, when your number was disconnected and there was no Nolan Forte on the internet, and my email sent to the band address got no response—I was hurt. And shocked. But I came to terms with it, you know?"

She'd been running her finger around the rim of her cup, but glanced up at him as she asked the question.

Nolan swallowed.

He forced himself to say nothing, and she glanced down again. "Then you showed up yesterday, and told me the truth, and that just confused everything. Like…

who are you?" Her gaze met his again. "You're making me not trust my own mind, my judgment, my heart, and that's not cool."

Oh, God. He should have stayed in New Orleans. He wasn't man enough to do this. To leave her in this state.

He saw now why Carmela had come to him. He'd taken a sweet, innocent woman and, in his own selfish need to preserve himself, had victimized her.

Or…he was falling prey to feelings that prompted him to think irrationally. Was he reading more into what she was saying, into what he'd done, as a justification to himself to see her again? To spend whatever time he could with her?

To what end?

Memories of Molly came flooding back. Not just her mind-set about her brother not hurting anyone by benefitting from knowing him, but earlier, too. Her lack of understanding of his commitment to the responsibility that came from his family's wealth. His need to please his family, to be there for them. To be a part of them.

And Molly hadn't even been predisposed to hate wealth. Lizzie had already stated, quite clearly, that she wanted no part of the type of life he led.

They could try, but resentment would build. And he couldn't bear to have last year's love turn to hate.

To hear Lizzie spew bitterness at him, as Molly had.

"I just needed to see you again," Lizzie said then, "to talk, to find out…"

It took everything Nolan had to remain seated and aloof as her voice faded off. She wanted to know if she was special to him. He could put her doubts to rest in a heartbeat.

As Nolan Forte.

Only to have to leave her again. Because he was Nolan Fortune.

He wanted to be honest with her. And tell her...what? That he was crazy about her, but knew better than to trust those wayward yearnings with himself? That he'd lived with them his entire life and knew they were his challenge, his temptation? That normally his music satisfied them completely, until he'd met her and the ante had been upped?

"My oldest brother, Austin, met a girl several years ago. Within a couple of weeks, he was certain she was the one and he married her."

"After knowing her two weeks?"

He nodded. They were looking at each other, eye to eye, talking. Just talking. Speaking and listening. With honest interest.

How in the hell could that feel like some kind of real connection? A year ago, yeah, they'd mixed sex in with the talking. But now?

"Wow," she said. "That's... Wow. Usually you just see stuff like that in the movies."

She smiled. And his brain just...paused.

For a second there, the tension between them was hiding. They were as they'd been last year.

"The marriage didn't last."

Lizzie frowned. "He didn't really love her?"

"He didn't really even know her," he said, taking a sip of his coffee, as though that could somehow distract him from the intensity dancing between them. But what happened with his brother's whirlwind romance was only a small part of Nolan's reasons for leaving her. She'd told him that she needed to understand.

And he knew what he had to give her.

"I thought I was in love once before," he told her. "In

college. I was away from the family, away from anyone who knew me. I was a regular guy, kind of like Nolan Forte. I blended in. And I met a girl."

Her face froze. He'd not known, until that moment, that expressions really could be like stone.

"So this is just what you do? Pretend you're someone else and fall in love for a short period of time?"

What? Wait! "No!" He sat forward, reached for her arm when she moved as though she was going to take her tea and walk. "It's that I've made mistakes and am leery of making them again." He could hear the passion in his voice, but couldn't take time at the moment to edit it out. "Molly truly seemed like the one for me. But it turned out that our views on life were so vastly different that everyone got hurt." He was simplifying. Giving a really bad year of his life in two sentences.

"So you just decided for both of us that we wouldn't work, without even giving me a chance. You just bailed."

"I'm sorry, Lizzie. I just…it was two weeks. How well can you really know someone in two weeks? You can feel like you do, the temptation can definitely be there and make you think you're doing the right thing, but…" He tossed up a hand.

"Is that why you pose as Nolan Forte? So you can indulge your need to be with a 'regular' woman, without ever having the time for it to develop into a real relationship?"

Her question was calm, quiet, sounding almost… compassionate. "No," he said. It was his job to sort his truths from his wishes or wants. To keep them apart. "I'm Nolan Forte for a purely selfish reason, but not that one. For occasional weekends, and these two weeks over Christmas, I get to live without responsibility. That's it. Plain and simple and not real pretty."

She nodded, but didn't look as horrified as she should have. "So that's where I fell into your life…the no-responsibility part."

Yep. He nodded, knowing he should be relieved that she fully got it now. But he felt compelled to add, "You were special to me, Lizzie. Our time was…the best vacation I've ever had. I don't want you to ever think that you were just one of a bunch, or that I've ever had any relationship like the one we shared last year."

"But you knew all along that there was no chance it would be more than that."

He nodded again.

"So why give me a phone number?"

"I was caught up in the moment…not thinking clearly."

"So wait a minute. The number you left…it was a real one?"

He couldn't let the hope on her face take root. "I have a cell that I use only for band contact. That's the number I gave you. And the number I changed."

"Nolan Forte's number."

"Right."

"You never intended me to know, even for a second last year, even when you gave me that number, that you were Nolan Fortune. If I'd seen you again, it would have been as Nolan Forte."

He let his shameful truth lay there between them.

Lizzie's stomach was in knots. Her heart felt as if it was on a roller-coaster ride, and she couldn't seem to catch up with herself. Sitting there with Nolan, it was like a force inside of her was trying to grasp for something that was just out of reach.

He'd intended to deceive her all along.

But the man she'd fallen for seemed to exist. Sort of.

He'd come back when Carmela compelled him to do so. Because he'd thought Lizzie needed him. Nolan Forte had been a man of integrity.

He'd also changed his phone number, leaving her no way to contact him. Nolan Fortune put his wealthy family, his position in that family, first.

From that she quickly guessed two things. If Nolan Forte found out about Stella, he would insist on taking responsibility. And Nolan Fortune could very well sue her for custody.

He had a fortune. She did not.

How could she possibly hope to fight high-priced lawyers and a family who could so obviously provide her daughter with so much more than she could? At least by worldly standards.

They couldn't take her baby away from her. There were no grounds. She was a good mother.

But they could probably force her to keep Stella close to them, to let them have her half the time. And what kid would rather be in a two-bedroom apartment with the bare minimum rather than in a princess room in a palace?

They could use what they had to turn her head away from what mattered most in life. Just as Nolan's head had been turned. If what he'd told her was true, he'd been as much in love with her as she'd been with him the year before. But the family money had won out.

Visions of home in Chicago, of being alone with sitters while her parents flitted about with the Mahoneys, sprang to mind. The crushing sense of loneliness filled her.

You're exactly what I want to be...pursuing a career you love with passion, rather than being driven by

*wealth. I know not many would agree with me, but I feel
sorry for insanely rich people. They're in a prison from
which they'll never escape, being controlled by money.
It exacts everything from you, but will leave you in an
instant if you make a wrong move.*

Her words from the year before came back to her.
They'd described Nolan Forte. Little did she know they
also described Nolan Fortune. He was in that prison.

Could she bear to allow that to happen to her sweet
Stella?

One thing she knew for certain: she couldn't trust
Nolan Fortune to do what was best for either her or
Stella. He'd do what was best for the Fortunes.

"Let's take a walk," she said, suddenly in a prison of
her own in that coffeehouse, trapped in a chair across
from the father of her baby, the probable love of her life
and a man she neither knew well nor respected all that
much. She was trying to decide her daughter's entire
future in a split second.

She couldn't figure out the two weeks in which Stella
had been conceived. How could she possibly make
choices that would change a soul's entire destiny?

She needed time. More than she'd have obviously,
but any would be better than none. Time to figure him
out, to be with Nolan Fortune, as himself, and see how
much of Nolan Forte was alive in there. Time to get her
own mind and heart wrapped around the truth of the
affair she'd had with an imaginary man.

And yet, a man so real she ached to touch him, to be
touched by him, even now.

She needed time to hold her baby close, quiet her
mind and find peace in her heart.

"I'm sorry," Nolan said, still beside her, though

they'd walked a block from the coffee shop and she hadn't said a word.

"I know." She wasn't heading anywhere in particular. The area around campus was filled with shops and eateries, bars, apartments and homes, too. Sunday in December gave the streets added flair, with Christmas decorations, traffic, shopping frenzy and early celebrations.

He asked her about her graduation, and was glad to know her aunt had made it down for the ceremony. He wanted to know about her current job. Wished she were able to work in her field of music, rather than substitute, but was sure her students were benefitting from having her with them.

It was rhetoric, she knew that, and absorbed it like cotton taking on water. Nolan's praise was on a line straight to her heart. Not good.

And yet, it was a reality she'd have to face if she was going to be a good mother.

She didn't ask him a single question about his life. At the moment, she was too busy struggling to put one foot in front of the other and form coherent answers to his questions—while her mind floundered with a million questions of her own.

Ten minutes from the coffee shop, Nolan touched her elbow. "What's that over there?"

In a park diagonally across the street from them, a small band was setting up in front of a gathering of folded chairs. "You want to go see?" he asked.

The year before they'd happened upon Christmas carolers one night. They'd followed them for a bit and then had ended up joining in, singing harmony as though they'd rehearsed for months. The entire gang had shown up at the pub the next night to hear Nolan play.

No way should she walk back down any memory lanes. "Yeah," she said. Only to buy herself time, she hoped, but feared she was lying to herself.

There was a sax, a flute and a clarinet—all wind instruments. Her personal favorites. Which was what had drawn her to Nolan Forte in the first place. He was a gifted saxophone player.

"Does Nolan Fortune ever play the sax?" she asked as they wandered over and took seats in the back of about ten rows. The rest of the rows were filling rapidly, as though people knew the band was going to be there and had planned to attend, as opposed to just happening upon the moment as she and Nolan had done.

All they'd ever done. Things happened. There was no planning.

Had been no planning.

She couldn't live like that anymore. She had Stella to consider. Bills to pay. A life to figure out.

"I play pretty much every day. Mostly late at night," he said, glancing over at her. Her mind had been spinning so fast she'd almost forgotten the question.

He played every day. Letting Nolan Forte live and breathe. Her heart took hope. But he played mostly late at night. Because that was the only time he could squeeze out for the heart and soul of him? Because, even for himself, the heart came last?

As she pondered those questions, the three band members, middle-aged men in red sweaters and black jeans, were taking up their instruments, obviously ready to begin.

There were no mics. No introductions. Just notes filling the air. Really filling it. Sweetly. Powerfully.

Expecting traditional Christmas songs, Lizzie was caught up in a tune she'd never heard before. With the trebles and bass notes, the perfectly placed pianissimos, the song evoked a longing in her she couldn't contain. It built, welled, and when Nolan took her hand toward the end, she held on, even after the music died away and applause erupted. Then a version of "Santa Claus Is Coming to Town" started, and she pulled away, clasping her hands together in her lap and pushing them between her thighs for added safety. Even then, she felt the chords washing over her and she wanted to sing along. And then, with the next song, to lose herself again. To become one with the angels and fly with joy. To know that great sacrifice, hard work, led to happiness. To believe that love really was the most powerful force of all.

When the half hour concert was over, she had to sit for a minute, still absorbing the impact of the music.

"That was magnificent." Nolan's soft tone was almost reverent. He'd made no move to stand, either. And then, a full minute later, he said, "I can't believe they're playing a free concert in the park. They should be recording."

She stood, not wanting to hear anymore. She couldn't bear for him to spoil the moment with a shift from the godly gift they'd just shared, to monetary wealth. To her, such great talent, being used for a free concert in the park, was perfection.

To Nolan Fortune, it was a waste.

And this was the man she had to share her daughter with?

She couldn't do it.

She had to do it.

God help her, she didn't know what to do. She wanted to hide Stella until he was gone and never tell either of them. There were moments when she truly thought it would be best for Stella. She was petrified at the thought of the changes wealth would bring to her daughter's perspectives.

And yet, did she have a choice?

Nolan was Stella's father. She was already a Fortune. Nothing was going to change that.

Chapter Eight

Nolan played his set on Sunday night, pouring his frustration into music that, when he closed his eyes, took him to a place where he was real.

But he was constantly searching the room for the woman who had the power to ruin him. He couldn't seem to get her out of his system.

Even with all of the tension his lies had caused between them, he'd been happier with her than he was apart.

Monday morning, lying in bed, he told himself that he had to let it go. Let *her* go. Showered and dressed in the jeans he wanted to wear, he called off of breakfast with his bandmates and headed away from the hotel. He walked with purpose.

He ended up at Lizzie's door in near-record time. They had ten days. Maybe, with truth standing between them, they wouldn't enjoy each other as much. Wouldn't even like each other. Maybe she wouldn't want to see him again, in spite of the unfinished business that had prompted her to call him the day before.

After the concert in the park he'd had to head back to the hotel, to get ready for a short rehearsal and then dinner before the night's gig. There'd been no time for closure.

He'd bent to kiss her cheek. She'd turned at just that moment, probably to say goodbye, and their lips had met. Clearly an accident. They'd both pulled back at once.

But his appetite had been whetted.

Based on the confused and longing look in her gaze, hers had, too.

Staring up at her window now, he told himself he was being a fool. He thought of Molly, of all that he'd learned, the pain he had to avoid, for both him and Lizzie.

But she'd called him out on the way he'd taken the choice from her the year before, when he made the decision to cut them off from each other without telling her why. Without giving her half the choice. If she wanted another ten days, if she needed them anywhere nearly as badly as he did, did he have the right to refuse her? Didn't he owe her?

He took a step up the walk toward her front door.

They could have a no-sex rule. Just be friends. With each other. And with the truth.

Uh-huh. They could try.

Confidence filled him as he knocked. The worst she could do was tell him to leave.

And then he'd be free.

Yes. At peace with his decision, he knocked a second time. Her car was in the lot and schools were closed for Christmas break, so she should be home. She could be in the shower.

He could have called but he'd purposely chosen not to. He needed to see her face-to-face. Either to say goodbye or another hello.

The lock on the door clicked, and he stepped back, a smile on his face. Lizzie, in gray sweats and a wrinkled T-shirt, slipped outside, leaving him barely a glimpse of the home he'd been so completely comfortable in the year before.

"Nolan! You can't keep just stopping by like this."

Not, "You have to leave." Or even, "Why are you here?"

With a shrug, he shoved his fingers into the front pockets of his jeans so that he didn't do something stupid like reach out to run them over her lips. "I can go away and call if you want. I wondered if you'd like to have lunch? Anywhere you choose." It was the Nolan Fortune way. "Seriously, I'd like to spoil you like crazy." Take her shopping. Buy her whatever she wanted. Because he hadn't been able to do so the year before.

Because she deserved the best of whatever she wanted.

"I can't. I have to get back in," she said, glancing back at the door. "I, uh, have a bath running."

She had bed hair and no makeup, not that she wore much.

"That's cool," he said, nodding. "So how about lunch tomorrow?"

She frowned, looked pained, and he braced for the refusal, and perhaps a final goodbye. "Maybe." Another glance back. "Can I call you?" She'd turned the knob, was pushing back inside the door.

"Of cour—"

Nolan's happy agreement broke off as an unmistakable wail sounded behind Lizzie—from inside that apartment.

"Are you babysitting?" he asked. Earning money during her holiday?

"Yes!" The word came out, along with a complete change in her. "Yes, I am." She smiled at him and opened the door more completely, not to invite him in, but just as if she had nothing to hide.

And with a flash, Carmela's expression the other night when she'd faced him at the bar sprang to mind.

You messed her up, Forte.

Yet, when he'd seen her, other than being understandably wary and pissed at him, she hadn't seemed messed up at all. She'd graduated. Had a job.

Suddenly the fear he'd seen in her eyes a couple of times took on all new significance.

Oh, God.

"Do you really have a bath running?" She seemed to have forgotten about it and water could be running over.

He hoped to God water was running over. And that she was babysitting.

"No."

She'd lied. His senses honed, the rest of him was nebulous.

"Who are you babysitting for?" His entire system just kind of paused. He felt nothing. Like he'd been put on ice for a future thaw.

The stricken look that came over her face could have been missed if he hadn't been watching her so closely. "Carmela," she said then, in that overcheery voice. "Didn't she tell you? She has a baby."

"Carmela."

"Yes! She has a baby. Isn't that great?"

"Is she home?"

"No! I told you, I'm babysitting. She's working today. She's an intern for an architectural firm."

The baby let out another wail, obviously agitated, and Lizzie looked behind her.

"You better go tend to that," Nolan said, still standing there.

She nodded, and as she closed the door, she said, "I'll call you about tomor—" But Nolan, all Fortune now, stepped forward. He didn't enter her home, but her words broke off as his foot kept the door from closing.

"I can wait," he said.

"Nolan…"

The baby's cries became more urgent, even to an untrained idiot like him.

He could be wrong.

Had to be wrong.

She'd tried to call him months ago. And when she'd been unable to reach him, she had been frantic enough to try to track him through the band.

And then Carmela had sought him out at the club.

What friend looked up a guy a year later after he'd supposedly duped her friend, saying he had to go see her?

The woman had had an almost desperate urgency about her in the bar the other night.

Every nerve tight to the point of pain, Nolan stood there on the doorstep, watching as Lizzie moved out of sight, going farther into the living room, which he knew from his previous occupancy of the apartment.

The crying stopped almost immediately.

"It's okay, baby girl, I'm right here." He heard her voice, a tone he didn't recognize and yet reacted to fiercely with a melting inside that he couldn't prevent.

And then she was back, his Lizzie, holding a tiny

little body with flailing arms and the biggest, roundest wide-open brown eyes that were staring right at him.

Through him.

The pink one-piece thing had hearts all over it. Varying sizes, some white, some yellow, some a darker pink. He couldn't stop staring at those hearts.

Pink. A girl?

He wanted to ask what Carmela had named her baby, how long Lizzie would be babysitting, but the truth wasn't letting him breathe, let alone talk.

"Her name's Stella," Lizzie said, cradling the little thing who seemed perfectly content now that she was being held.

A girl. A baby girl.

Nolan wasn't sure how long he stood there, staring at the hearts. Too long, for sure.

Finally he turned to go, then turned back, intending to say a ton, came up empty and turned away again. He made it to the edge of the parking lot. Turned back and double-timed it to the door.

Lizzie still stood there, holding that baby. He looked her in the eye. Brown eyes, like the baby's. And like his, too.

"She's yours," he said.

Her nod confirmed what he already knew.

"And mine." The last word stuck in his throat.

Lizzie neither confirmed nor denied his assertion. Nolan was fixated on the round chubby cheeks, the big brown eyes that seemed to know him as well as he knew himself, a little bird mouth that he imagined had a lot to say.

"There are no tears on her cheeks," he said inanely. She'd been crying so hard.

"She was just mad because she woke up in the swing and couldn't see anyone. That was her mad cry."

She had a mad cry. Lizzie recognized it when she heard it.

He couldn't look at Lizzie. At the mother of that baby who hadn't said that the child was his.

"I have a daughter." The words were so unreal they didn't seem to have any effect on him at all.

This time she replied. "Yes."

Starting to shake from the inside out, he looked up at Lizzie. He saw a wealth of love—not for him—and fear—because of him?—and said the only thing he could. "May I come in?"

Stella started to fuss even before the door closed behind Nolan. As if she could truly sense her mother's state of mind, as some experts said babies could do. More likely, she could feel the trembling Lizzie was trying desperately to control. There were two full bottles in the fridge, and frozen breast milk in the freezer, too, but Stella wasn't usually content to take a bottle whenever Lizzie was around.

Grabbing the baby's favorite pacifier, she offered it up, and sent up a quick word of thanks when Stella suckled contentedly. The baby wasn't due to eat again for another hour or so. But that could fluctuate an hour either way, too. She was keeping Stella on a baby-driven schedule at the advice of her pediatrician and based on the reading she'd done. As much as she could, anyway, with her and Carmela's schedules. Carmela, who'd been to a few of their doctor appointments, supported her choice.

Would Nolan?

Would his family try to intervene? To determine that some other way was better for the child? Try to force formula on her so that Stella wasn't as dependent on Lizzie?

Rocking the baby softly as she walked, she told herself to get a grip. If she went nuts she'd be no good to Stella at all.

Nolan was sitting on the edge of one end of the couch, hands folded, thumbs rubbing back and forth against each other. He seemed to be honing in on the blank TV screen, but every other second or so, he'd glance at the baby swing.

Feeling a little less rattled, Lizzie lifted a dozing Stella up onto her shoulder, and joined him in the living room—taking the chair farthest from the couch.

"I'm sorry for how I look," she said softly, not wanting to rouse Stella. "I was planning to shower while she napped." His glance finally turned her way, and she wished like hell that she'd kept her mouth shut.

Why hadn't she just been silent?

What did one do when the father of one's child showed up suddenly on one's doorstep and found out he was a father?

She took control, that's what. Stella was depending on her to take care of this situation.

"I don't want anything from you," she said, putting every ounce of classroom authority she could muster into her tone. "You purposely aren't named on the birth certificate so you needn't worry that I'll come after you later. And I'll sign anything you need me to sign relinquishing you of any responsibility." Once the words started, they just rolled off her tongue, as though all of those months, thinking about what she'd say to him if she ever saw him, had been rehearsal for now.

"When I found out I was pregnant there was time to terminate easily, medically speaking, and with little risk. Adoption was always an option, too. On my own, I knowingly made the conscious decision to have her, to keep her, to become a single mother. I chose to take on this adventure and I hold no one but myself accountable to it."

There. Good. She was in control. The boss.

"I have a daughter."

Sounding more shocked than threatening, Nolan looked right at her. Lizzie, feeling threatened, said nothing.

"I'm a father."

"Biologically speaking." Yes. Right. She could do this. Stella sighed, her pacifier slipping down the back of Lizzie's shoulder as those tiny lips let go. Lizzie rocked her.

Nolan blinked. And seemed to change, right there before her eyes. It was like someone had opened up a spout and all kinds of emotion came pouring out. His gaze was personal, warm, to the point of melting her insides. Nolan Fortune was gone and Nolan Forte had entered the room. Not really, she knew that, but for a second there, she was in love again.

But only for a second.

"I don't know what to say." He just sat there, rubbing his hands, staring, while his expression changed. And changed again. His eyes had grown moist. Her heart lurched. She'd had weeks to come to terms with reality before she'd really even started to show. Months before her life had irrevocably changed.

He was getting the full deal in a matter of seconds.

"You don't have to say anything," she assured him, calming as she realized that she truly did have the upper hand. "This has to be a shock, but really, Nolan, nothing in your life has to change. It's not like she suddenly just landed on earth. She's been here three months, we've been doing just fine, and will continue to do so. I'm happy. Truly happier than I've ever been."

Except maybe during some of those most incredible moments with him the year before. She'd touched true joy for the first time the night he'd held her in his arms.

"I…" He just sat there, watching her.

Lizzie didn't want to be rude, but she really did have to get on with her day. Take her shower. Do some laundry. Change the sheets. Make dinner for Carmela. Feed the baby several times in between it all.

Cry a bit, now that Nolan knew.

"I don't know how to hold a baby." His hands stilled. "I've never held one. We don't… None of my siblings have kids yet."

"You don't need to hold her."

"I think I do."

No. Really. He didn't.

"I meant what I said, Nolan. You don't have to do anything here."

"I think I do."

Okay, it was going bad fast. She had to stop it somehow.

"What is it you think you have to do?" She had to know what she was defending against before she'd know how to do it.

"I have no idea."

Good. Somehow she had to keep it that way. Still, her wayward heart cried for him. Reached out to him. She hadn't meant for him to be hurt.

She hadn't meant to be pregnant in the first place. They'd used condoms. Every time.

"She doesn't need you to do anything, Nolan," she said, trying to soften her words enough to make them sound as kind as she intended. They were just fine without him.

So why did she feel a sudden stab of guilt as she felt her daughter sigh against her again, so trustingly.

What if Stella wanted Nolan to do something? What if she needed more than Lizzie could give her as a single schoolteacher mom?

What if his family had a wealth of love, in addition to an overflowing bank of money, to offer her?

"Can I touch her?" He stood and approached her chair, so Lizzie stood, too.

"What do you mean?"

He reached out a hand. "I just want to…touch her." His hand stopped inches from the baby's back. "Can I?"

He was her father! "Of course," she said, because there was no other option.

His hand came closer, and then stopped again. Nolan looked at Lizzie. "She's so small. I don't want to hurt her."

"It's fine," she said, her heart taking over as she lifted her own hand to his and placed it gently on Stella's tiny back. "She likes to have her back rubbed," she said softly, moving his fingers in a slow circular motion. "Gently, like that," she said, then dropped her hand.

His movement stopped for a second and then started again. Rubbing gently in the same exact circle Lizzie had started him with. Over and over. Just rubbing.

Maybe he wasn't ever going to stop.

The thought was ludicrous, but the man seemed so engrossed. So completely lost to his endeavor.

Tears sprang to her eyes. She didn't mean them to. Didn't want them to. And yet, there they were, blurring her vision, and she knew, life had just changed.

Irrevocably.

Again.

Chapter Nine

He'd made Lizzie cry. And made the baby cry, too, apparently, as she'd started to squirm and wail right when he was rubbing her back. Having taken that as his clue to excuse himself, he'd hightailed it out of the apartment.

Lizzie had said Stella needed to eat.

He needed time to think.

He didn't get more than a couple of blocks away from the apartment before he was bombarded by his own questions. When was she born? How old was she? Oh, right. Lizzie had said she was three months. Quickly counting the months since their last night together, he came up with that same answer. Three months, give or take a week or two.

How had Lizzie managed, alone, pregnant and in school? Was there debt? He'd settle that immediately.

Had she been all alone at the birth?

How long did it take an infant to eat?

He gave it half an hour, pacing back and forth between Lizzie's apartment and the coffee shop they'd frequented, last year and this.

She'd called him after he'd left her last year.

Because of Stella.

He was a father.

His mom and dad were grandparents.

Oh, God.

He couldn't think of them right now. Couldn't think of the family.

He was the youngest son, and the first to produce an heir to the family fortune. The thought gave him a stupid little thrill.

It lasted all of two seconds and then the sick feeling of dread, accompanied by a weight he had no idea how to carry, descended on him again. Accompanied by just a hint of something more.

Something…beyond good. It was nebulous. Completely out of reach. But hanging there.

He was a father. Forevermore there'd be another human being in the world that he'd helped create.

With Lizzie.

His yearning had become his coparent.

Who wanted nothing to do with him. Wanted nothing from him.

In fact, she wanted him out of her life. And Stella's, too.

Nolan wanted to give her whatever she wanted, but he couldn't walk away from them. Maybe physically he could put distance between them. Maybe. But they were his responsibility. His family now. And family was everything.

As that one thought settled, he headed back up to Lizzie's door. When she answered his knock, almost immediately, holding his sleeping daughter, he didn't hesitate as he said, "We need to talk."

As though she'd expected him, maybe had even been watching for him, she nodded, pulled open the door and settled back in her chair in the living room, tucking her bare feet up into the cushion with her.

"Do you need to put her down?" he asked.

That small bundle, the sweet pudgy face with closed eyes and that tiny little puckered mouth—it made him speechless. And he had a lot he had to say.

"She'll sleep better if I hold her," Lizzie said. He had no idea if she was speaking the truth, half wondered if holding the baby gave her some kind of edge over him, and figured, if it did, she deserved it.

"She looks perfect," he said, dropping back down to the edge of the couch, his hands on his thighs. They seemed out of place, having nowhere to hang. Nothing to do.

They were too empty.

And easier to focus on than anything else in that room.

"She is perfect." The love in Lizzie's voice was audible.

And heartrending. He'd lost his chance to be a part of this little trio from the beginning. To be a partner to her in bringing their child into the world. She'd called him and he'd made himself completely unattainable.

"So...she's healthy? There were no problems? With her birth, I mean. Or the pregnancy?"

He'd missed the first year of his daughter's life. The fetal stage. And everything that came between then and the sleeping baby across from him.

Lizzie's silence ratcheted up the tension inside him.

"What's her birthday?"

"September 23."

Nine people in his family—seven siblings and their parents—and they had no September birthdays.

"She'll be three months old next week," Lizzie added, giving him information he could figure for himself when what he needed were real details. All of them.

Though he probably didn't deserve them. He'd had his chance. She'd tried to find him.

"How long were you in labor?"

He had no personal experience, but he'd seen television and knew the basics. Labor looked excruciating—something he'd never understood a guy putting a woman he loved through. Figured, when it came that time for him, he'd have better understanding.

"Not long."

Thank God. "You had her quickly, then?"

She shrugged. Kind of nodded.

"Did you have a coach?"

"No."

"Was Carmela there? Or your aunt?" He was immediately jealous of both of them.

"No."

Now he was put out by them. They'd left Lizzie all alone at such a critical time? As had he. The guilt was a strong acidy taste in his mouth. It made no difference that he hadn't known. He had no right to point fingers. No rights at all.

But he had responsibilities. Having no idea where that led him didn't let him off the hook.

"I can't believe Carmela wasn't there," he said, scrambling for his next move. Or word. "She—"

"Carmela got there as soon as she could." Lizzie's tone was unmistakably defensive as she interrupted him.

"You went that quickly?" He'd heard of that. There

was an episode of some sitcom where a woman gave birth in a cab or something. He couldn't quite remember.

"I had to have an emergency cesarean. That's why Carmela wasn't there. I wasn't even sure I was in labor. I had just gone into my doctor's office to have her check me, and my blood pressure was off the charts."

Her words, issued softly, almost as an afterthought, stabbed so deep.

"You were in danger?"

"I had a seizure at the doctor's office," she said, continuing to twist the blade of guilt inside him. "If they hadn't taken her I could have died. Or ended up with brain damage."

She could have had a seizure on the way to the doctor's office, been in a car crash. They both might have died.

Oh, God, what had he done? His damned selfish need to be free had driven him to make a woman pregnant. Fighting that yearning had left her alone to almost die.

"I'm so sorry, Lizzie." The words didn't even scrape the surface. "I should have been there. I'm so damned sorry."

"There's nothing you could have done. It came on suddenly. I'd just been in for a check earlier in the week because she was a couple of days late. Everything was fine. It was just one of those things."

"But you had major surgery... I... And caring for a newborn..." He had an entire family who'd have stepped in to help her. Three sisters and a mother who'd have known what to do.

And would've kicked him in the head on their way out the door, he was certain.

His family would love Stella. They weren't going to like what he'd done, however.

And they weren't going to be happy about Lizzie, either. They'd see her as another Molly, at least at first. And he couldn't blame them. Or maybe a Kelly. After Kelly, everyone was leery. The experience with Austin's wife had cost them all. Changed them all.

God, what had he done?

Ramifications closed in on him. He could just hear it now, him telling his family he'd impregnated a woman he'd only known a couple of weeks. A woman so far out of their normal social circle that if he hadn't been posing as Nolan Forte she'd never even have gotten close to him.

He'd have to tell them about his alter ego.

He could lose everything he held most dear—his time with the band and his family's respect, too.

But he'd gained something from which he could not walk away.

That little life over there. She was connected to him for all eternity.

She was going to need so much…deserved so much more. "I'm going to open a bank account," he told her. "In her name with you as trustee." He named a sum, a weekend's excursion to him, as starting money. "But until I can work that out…" He handed her a wad of cash that he'd pulled from his wallet. Safety cash in the event something catastrophic happened while he was on the road. "That's just what I can access immediately," he told her.

"No." Lizzie's tone was so sharp Stella stirred, started to cry. Her eyes blinked open and shut again almost immediately as Lizzie rocked and crooned to her. When the baby was sleeping soundly again, Lizzie looked over at Nolan.

"I'm not taking your money," she told him. "If you want to set up something for Stella for later, a college fund or something, I can't stop you. But I will not be beholden to you financially."

He wasn't going to "own" her, he translated, feeling stupid standing there holding his wad of cash.

And because of all the talks they'd had the year before, her lack of desire to ever even play the lottery because she didn't want to take a chance on winning money and having it change her life, he understood.

No one else would believe him, though. They'd think she was working him. That the amount he'd named hadn't been enough.

He put his cash away, but he was still opening the account as soon as he got home. It was the right thing to do. All money wasn't dirty. And all people with it weren't ruled by it. His big, boisterous, argumentative and inarguably loving family was proof of that.

"I can't just walk away, Lizzie."

Her shrug, the way she pulled the baby even closer, prepared him for her response. "You did it once, Nolan, I'm sure you can manage a second time. I have your number now. I can call if I run into some kind of world-ending financial emergency."

Cruelty wasn't her way.

Which told him she was scared.

Thing was, he completely understood. Commiserated. He was pretty terrified himself.

He just couldn't give her what she wanted. He couldn't walk out of her life and leave her alone with Stella.

Whether she deserved it or not.

Chapter Ten

She was going to have to do something. Come up with a plan. Short of changing her identity and leaving the country. The only way she'd have the means to do that would be if she actually took some of the money Nolan Fortune was throwing around.

He'd offered her more, for starters, liquid in an account immediately, than she'd make in a year of teaching full-time. More than she'd probably ever manage to save, let alone be able to give away like he was, while Stella was growing up.

I can't just walk away, Lizzie...

She wanted him out of her living room and her snarky comment hadn't worked to that end. He was still sitting there, watching her and Stella like they were the last meal on earth.

Didn't he have enough already? His family. His fortune. His Fortune family... The thought struck her almost hysterically.

Until she remembered that, technically, biologically, Stella was a Fortune, too.

And they were all about family.

With enough money to get whatever and whoever they wanted. He'd already been throwing it around. Should she take it so she'd have the resources to fight him with?

Could she use his money to hire a lawyer?

But she was pretty sure one payment wouldn't be enough. They'd just keep coming at her until she was destitute.

Feeling like she had the entire world of moneyed people pressing at her back, she started to panic, and knew she had to find a way to stave them off. To find a safe place for her and Stella.

At least until she could figure out the sane thing to do. What was best for Stella.

"I want to give you everything you want and need," Nolan said after several minutes of silence. "I just can't give you this, Lizzie. I can't walk away."

He was going to leave her apartment, though. Sooner or later. And when he did, would he be on the phone to his people before he even left her block? Would he be calling out the guards?

Did he have a bodyguard outside even now?

Wealthy people traveled with them, didn't they? Not that she'd seen any the previous year. Of course, they could have been disguised as—

No!

She had to stop these crazy thoughts. She had to take control. To buy herself some time to figure this out. If only she could hold him hostage in the apartment long enough for her to get some divine intervention.

No, she didn't want that—him hostage there with her. She couldn't afford to keep Nolan close.

He kept giving her glimpses of Forte and they were messing with her. Making her weak. Making her want him as badly as she wanted him gone.

But...

"You really mean that about giving me whatever I want?" she asked, looking him straight in the eye.

"Except for walking out on the two of you again? Absolutely."

"Then this is the deal I've got for you." She rushed on ahead before she could second-guess herself. "You're here for ten more days, right?"

"Give or take."

Did the man ever have a straight answer?

"I'm expected home for Christmas Day, but in light of...this... I'm not sure I'm going..."

He'd been expected home the year before, too, but she couldn't dwell on the past.

"Okay, so here's what I want and what I'm prepared to give to get it." Rich people were into deals, right? "I want you to refrain from telling anyone, and I mean anyone, about Stella being yours for the next ten days. I'll agree to spend as much or as little time with you as you please—with Stella, of course. I'm not offering up myself. Let's make that very clear. We'll spend time together to see if we can work out some kind of amicable plan where the future is concerned. You'll be able to get to know her if you want, to spend time with her. I'm on break from teaching until after the first of the year, so I'll put no time limits on your exposure to us, and we can try to talk this all through. Slowly. With time on both sides for thinking." Holy moly, divine intervention really existed? She'd sounded...mature. Best of all, she'd sounded in charge. In control. Like she was the one with the power to call the shots.

Keeping her head high, her gaze on him, she felt a little bit like sticking her chin out. But she was shaking inside too much to give it a try. She didn't want her facade to crumble in front of him. She was going to have to surrender Stella to a life of partial wealth, which made her feel as though her whole world was crumbling.

And yet…having Nolan there, in their home, God, it felt good.

"Deal."

He'd taken about three seconds to think about it.

"You're sure? No calls to anyone."

"No calls." He smiled. "I think it's a great plan, Lizzie. I'd welcome the time, to tell you the truth."

Time with her and Stella? Or time before he called home?

Did it matter? She'd bought herself and Stella some time with Nolan Forte. Time to figure out how to deal with Nolan Fortune and the rest of his powerful people.

"Okay, then," she said as she stood. "Since I didn't get to it yesterday, my agenda for today was to get this place decorated for Christmas. You up for that?"

His grin just about knocked her back into her chair. She felt it flow through her body and puddle in her crotch.

"Lead on," he said, standing. And then, his gaze intently on Stella, he added, "If you want to take that shower I can sit and watch her. You know, call out to you if she wakes up or anything."

"You want to hold her?" She held her daughter close, not ready for that big of a step yet. Not ready to hand her over. Even for a second.

"No. I was… You'd said you were going to bathe

while she slept. I figured, if you didn't mind, I'd watch her sleep."

Such a sweet, simple request. And yet, she hesitated.

"Or, if you'd rather, I can wait outside…"

"I was… I just… Her Pack 'n Play is in my room. That's where she sleeps when I shower."

Unless she was in her swing. But she had to fall asleep there or it wouldn't work.

"Good, fine," he said, backing toward the door. "How about if I walk down and get us some coffee and muffins?"

He was letting her make the rules. For now. He was a smart man, though. She couldn't afford to underestimate him. Couldn't afford to get comfortable. Who knew what kind of tricks men like him had in their cache of power plays?

"I, uh, don't drink coffee right now," she said. "I'm breastfeeding and the caffeine isn't good for her. But… decaf tea would be nice."

"With cream and a hint of cinnamon like you ordered it yesterday," he said, at the door now.

"Yes."

"Be back in a few," he said, letting himself out.

He was gone before she remembered to thank him.

For the rest of that afternoon Nolan noticed the energy in his step—the sense of adventure alive and well inside of him. He was revved up. Ready to take on the world.

He was falling back into the trap of the year before. Living for the moment. Knowing the end date before he even began. He saw it happening.

Allowed it to happen.

Ignoring the intense feeling Lizzie created within

him hadn't been the right choice. He most definitely should not have changed his number, or left her no way to contact him.

She'd given them ten days to find the right choice. He was up for that.

Ten days to figure out how they were going to be a family before he had to face his family. She'd acted like she was asking him for some great favor, keeping their secret until after Christmas. Truth was, he was dreading laying this one on the old man.

Like it or not, his family meant everything to him. He had ten days to figure out how to make this all right. To find a way to provide for Lizzie and Stella and not lose the respect of his parents and siblings.

Maybe if he just kept his new little family secret, as he had Nolan Forte all these years, at least until enough time had passed for him and Lizzie to test just how being in each other's lives might look.

His parents were still going to be disappointed in him. He knew better than to go around getting women pregnant. Fortunes had responsibilities and keeping track of one's sperm was one of them.

"You sure she's going to be fine with a tree up?" Nolan asked Lizzie later that afternoon as she directed him to a four-by-six-foot storage area in the back of the front closet where she and Carmela stored their Christmas bins. In one of them was an artificial tree that needed to be put together.

"Why wouldn't she be?" she asked, rocking back and forth on her feet with a wide-awake baby in her arms. Stella was going to need to eat again soon, which meant she was going back to her bedroom. She wanted Nolan fully occupied with enough to keep him busy for the half hour it could take if their daughter chose to lollygag.

"I don't know…it might fall over," he said, coming out with the largest of the green-lidded bins. The one with the tree.

"I'm not planning to lay her under it," she told his way too cute butt as he bent over to access the storage area again.

Pushing a smaller bin out and placing another one on top of it, he paused to glance over at Lizzie and the baby.

"Yeah," he said. "Right."

"She's little and fragile, Nolan, but at the same time, she's a lot more durable than you'd think," she told him, breaking into a smile that felt free. Natural.

Better than she'd been in just about…a year.

Just because she'd bought herself a week before she really had to worry. And because she'd always felt magic in the air when the Christmas bins came out. Like miracles were possible.

She really wanted to believe that it had nothing to do with Nolan being back.

The baby turned her head, opening her mouth over Lizzie's T-shirted breast. Of course Nolan would look at them right then. And stand there and stare.

"Um, I'll just go back and feed her," she said, figuring it would be best to get it started before Stella cried. "If you want, you can start on the tree. It goes under the window." There was only one of them in the living area. A big, double window looking out at a lovely landscaped courtyard. Her bedroom, down the hall and on the other side of the apartment, looked at the parking lot.

A good dose of reality for her, she figured as she turned her back abruptly and started down the hall.

Should she close her door? She and Carmela never

closed doors unless one or the other of them had a guy in the apartment. Which was pretty much never, other than Nolan the previous year, and Carmela had been gone for a lot of that time.

She pushed it mostly closed. If he didn't glance down the hall, he'd never know she'd deliberately shut him out. Nolan might be Stella's father, but that didn't mean Lizzie had to invite him into their intimacies. Neither did she trust him to stay in the living room if she didn't make it clear he wasn't wanted.

Didn't trust herself to set boundaries if he strayed…

Taking her breast out, helping her daughter latch on, she couldn't help a surge of completely confusing and unwanted emotion. Feeding Stella was private and beautiful. Precious to the two of them. Having the baby's father in the house should make no difference to that.

But it did.

Ten minutes on one side and Stella was ready for the other breast. By that time Lizzie was ready to hide herself in the bathroom with the door locked.

Nolan knew what she was doing. Was probably picturing her and Stella right now. It wasn't like he hadn't seen her breasts before, she tried telling herself, to no avail.

Five minutes into the second half of her lunch Stella put her hand on the side of Lizzie's jaw. Of course Lizzie knew the action was purely accidental. The baby had no idea. And yet, the touch felt comforting. Like her daughter was reassuring her that all was well.

That she was enough.

"Liz?" Nolan's voice sounded like a ghost, whispering from the past. Except he was right outside her door. Her gaze shot in that direction, but the door was still resting against the jamb. He probably had a Christmas question.

"Yeah?"

"May I come in?"

"No!"

He didn't say anything else. She assumed he walked away. Maybe even out of the apartment.

She'd done the right thing, she assured herself as she wiped away tears.

Chapter Eleven

Nolan was just plugging in the lights he'd strung on the tree when Lizzie, carrying a wide-awake Stella, came back out to the living room. Almost as though he'd planned it, the colorful lights popped on just as they entered and Stella's gaze went immediately to the tree. The baby stared at it, while Nolan stared at them, the lights glistening in Stella's eyes, and Lizzie's, too.

It was a sight he'd never forget. A picture in a mental frame, the beautiful, natural-looking dark-haired woman holding the little pink bundle with big brown eyes. They were his responsibility forevermore. Whether Lizzie kicked him out of their lives, remarried, moved to Antarctica, it didn't matter. He owed her.

And Stella. He was going to support her. One way or another.

"I was thinking maybe we could go get some lunch," he said, the idea just occurring to him as he fought the urge to cross to his girls and take them both in his arms, beg their forgiveness and promise to never leave them again.

He couldn't do that. His life was in New Orleans. And that family was vital to him, as well. He was going to leave Austin. "Maybe at that pita place..."

Lizzie had loved it, even though she'd lamented, all three times they'd gone, that it was too expensive.

Looking from him to the tree and back, she nodded. "Then, when we get back, I'll help you with the rest of the decorations." They'd done that the year before, too, with her painting wonderfully cheerful mental images of memories of decorating the tree when she was a kid and her parents were still alive, down to the green and red candy-coated chocolate in the bowl on the coffee table.

He wasn't there to think about the past. Or to notice the lack of a candy-filled bowl in Lizzie's present.

She let him carry the oversize purse she used as a diaper bag out to her car. Everything else she handled herself, from strapping the baby into her car seat to driving to and from the restaurant. She held Stella the entire time they ate. And though she answered questions about feeding and sleeping schedules, about the babysitting arrangements she and Carmela had worked out, about the health insurance she carried on herself and the baby, provided in part by the school system, she gave him nothing unless he knew to ask for it.

She didn't offer to let him hold the baby. That first day, he didn't ask. He wasn't ready. He hung with them until he had to get back for a short rehearsal and the gig. He helped her finish her Christmas decorations, wanting to tell her about his own traditions at home— the way his siblings, every one of them, were home the day after Thanksgiving every year to help decorate the big tree in the living room of the family home. It was only one tree among many throughout the mansion, but that one big tree off the front foyer, that one they all did together. Still.

He didn't think Lizzie was open to stories about his family yet. She wasn't open to him at all.

Throughout that first afternoon he took photos of the baby on his phone, after asking permission and assuring Lizzie that they'd go nowhere but his own personal gallery.

That night, after the last set, he grabbed a beer from the market by the hotel, then went straight back to his hotel room and started scrolling through the pictures on his phone.

He couldn't seem to get enough. Of looking at her. Just knowing she was out in the world. Watching her. Being in the same room. Hearing her little baby sounds.

He'd recorded her crying shortly before he left. He was that far gone. Crying was her way of communicating, Lizzie had told him, and he'd just needed to have a record of the sound of her. Halfway through his beer, he played back the recording, over and over, and sat there grinning like a fool.

He had to swallow back unwanted emotion.

He was Stella's father.

But would he ever be her daddy?

Lizzie was playing a very risky game.

Regardless of Carmela telling her she was doing the right thing—giving Nolan time to become a father if he chose to do so and giving herself a chance to get to know the real Nolan Fortune so she could prepare herself for a future with him on the outskirts of her life—she barely slept Monday night.

She laid there, fighting memories of Nolan Forte. Of Christmas the year before.

She'd opened the door to his nearly constant presence in her life over the holiday this year, too. He'd said he wanted to spend every free minute he had with them. And the trouble was, she knew just how the ten days could look.

How she'd dreamed they could look.

A replica of the year before, but with their child as an added player. She'd fallen for him so completely before—let herself be convinced that the feelings he evoked in her were real. She'd believed in true love and the possibility of happily-ever-after.

And here they were, a year later, parents celebrating the holiday together with their infant daughter. If she wasn't careful, the picture was going to suck her in.

Because she couldn't quite convince herself that true love didn't exist.

What if…?

No. She had to keep reminding herself he'd already tried to make a Forte relationship work with the Fortunes. With Molly something or other. And look at how that turned out.

On Tuesday she insisted on shopping, figuring the safer bet was to be out in public. No more chances for intimate moments in her bedroom. Or anywhere else in her house.

She hadn't counted on Nolan insisting on paying for every single thing she tried to purchase. From diapers to a gift to send back to Chicago for her aunt. When she caught on, she simply quit shopping. And then was left with hours stretching before her. He suggested lunch at an upscale restaurant and then, before she knew what was happening, he'd taken the removable car seat carrier from her, slipped the handle over his forearm and waited for her to precede him inside.

The hostess thought they were a family. *No!* she wanted to scream. And she hated the warmth that suffused her system as other restaurant patrons watched them walk through to their table.

Because Stella was so cute, she told herself. Who didn't gush over a new baby?

But she knew differently. It was because Nolan Fortune was one of the hottest guys on the planet and the way he walked, like he not only owned the world but liked everyone in it, captivated attention.

In jeans and a red sweater, with cheap black boots, she told herself she looked like the hired help walking behind him. She couldn't convince herself to feel like it, though.

She felt like a cherished wife and mother.

For a moment. Only a moment.

That moment was too much for her.

No matter how nice Nolan was to her, how attentive to her and Stella, she couldn't fall for him again. His lavished attention had a definite end date. No matter what happened, he'd be rejoining his work-pressured world after the holiday.

He'd offered to give her money for the rest of her life. Not himself.

And even if he had offered her a permanent part in his life, she wasn't sure she'd want it. She just wasn't a girl who hankered after a prince or a knight in shining armor. She wanted a modest home, with three bedrooms and two bathrooms, a little backyard. A pet. And maybe, someday, a swimming pool. She wanted a husband who'd rush home from work to go with her to school concerts. And help with the dishes if she had papers to grade.

She wanted to teach music to kids who'd discover their own musical talents.

She wanted to raise her daughter herself. To be involved in all of the everyday changes in Stella's life. To get her hands dirty and make chocolate chip cookie mustaches.

She wanted the life the Mahoneys had stolen from her.

She wanted to lie in bed at night in a life she could control, feeling safe and secure.

She wanted Nolan to be a regular guy who'd think living in her imaginary three-bedroom house would be an honor.

But Nolan Fortune didn't even live on the same planet as that guy.

After he secured the carrier, with a sleeping Stella, in the high chair—he'd only watched Lizzie do it once the day before at the pita place—they sat down.

"If you're done shopping," he said, "I thought maybe this afternoon we could put Stella in her stroller and take her to Zilker Park. We won't be able to see the lights, since I have to be at the club before dark, but she can still see the huge tree. We could walk through the botanical garden, see the lake..."

They'd talked about visiting the park the year before but had never gotten around to it. "Are you sure you don't have other things to do?" she asked when her immediate response wanted to be *Yes, let's*. She had to spend this time with him. But she couldn't emotionally afford to enjoy it.

Getting over him the first time had nearly killed her.

Across the restaurant table, Nolan looked right into

her eyes, holding her captive. "Are you reneging on your deal?"

"Of course not. I just..." She was afraid. He hadn't mentioned the future since she'd offered to spend time with him. Hadn't opened any bank account that she knew of. Was dressing like the man she'd known. Acting like him. And sitting there with him, she wanted so badly to pretend he was the same man.

"I've got nine days," he said. "Every second counts."

She'd chosen to have his baby. To keep his baby after she gave birth. She'd opened this door.

Still looking him in the eye, she nodded. When she couldn't bear the intimate connection with him another second, she glanced at a sleeping Stella, and then studied her menu.

She had no idea what to order. Or how to find order in the chaos her life had become.

Nolan spent Wednesday, just seven days before Christmas, running errands with Lizzie. At the post office, where she dropped off the wrapped package for her aunt that they'd purchased the day before, he waited in the car with Stella sleeping in her car seat behind him. It was the first time he'd been alone with the little girl.

And Lizzie, whom he could see through the window of the post office, glanced out at them every few seconds. It was as though she wanted to make sure he wasn't taking off or in any other way interacting with the child he'd helped create.

Throughout the past couple of days, he'd caught glimpses of the woman who'd captivated him the year before, but her defenses were so high he was definitely hands-off.

He didn't need to be hands-on, he continuously told

himself. He needed only to solidify a plan to provide for her and their daughter. Leaving her defenses intact was the most righteous way to handle his association with her.

"How about a trip to the Santa Train today?" he asked when she returned to the car and suggested a fast-food hamburger place for lunch. The two-hour train ride, not as well known as the Austin Steam Train, because of it's expense for a mostly "kiddie" attraction, rode through hills decorated to look like little towns along the route to the North Pole, a mount that overlooked the city of Austin and hosted a five-star restaurant. It wasn't that he minded the burgers, but he only had nine more days to spoil her. Or maybe he was just fulfilling his own selfish need to be with her and be himself, too. "We could have lunch there." The Santa Train was one of a list of events and activities he'd collected off the internet the night before.

"What's the Santa Train?" she asked, frowning, as they sat in the post office parking lot with the car running. When he told her, her response was immediate. "I'm not dressed for even a three-star restaurant and I'm not sure about Stella. A long train ride seems like a lot…and it's not like she's old enough to enjoy the decorations or even know what's going on."

"If she's awake, she'll like the bright colors," he told her, thinking about the way the baby stared at Christmas tree lights, seemingly fascinated by them. "And if the motion of the train keeps her asleep, we can still enjoy them. And don't worry. Your jeans are perfect for a day in the hills, as are mine. If we look out of place, at least we'll do so together." He smiled at her.

She smiled back and he had to fight the urge to kiss her.

* * *

By the time they were rambling back down to Lizzie's car later that afternoon, Nolan buzzed with enough energy to propel the train himself. He'd spent himself silly in the gift shop, buying up every baby thing there. At first, Lizzie had joined in the game.

At what point she'd gone silent, he wasn't sure. She'd picked up the baby's carrier and walked out of the store. He'd been left carrying the bags filled with his purchases.

She'd perked up at lunch, laughing with him when he got Stella to smile and then laugh out loud by bringing his face close to hers over and over again and saying, "Boo!" He didn't notice the other patrons looking over, some with indulgent smiles, a couple with frowns, until Lizzie gave his foot a nudge under their table.

He'd been granted the honor of transporting the baby carrier out of the restaurant and back to the train, but only because Lizzie had taken the baby into the restroom to change and feed her. His gut leaped when the bathroom door opened twenty minutes later and she came walking out.

The Santa Train was an expensive treat for the rich and privileged. Beautiful people abounded around them. He'd watched many socialites walk out of the bathroom during the time he'd been waiting. Not one of them had elicited a response from his body.

Watching Lizzie walk toward him made his crotch swell, a fact he tried desperately to ignore as he held the carrier while she latched the baby inside.

And then they were on the ride out of the hills, speeding back to a reality he didn't want to embrace.

"I can swing two weekends here a month if I quit the band." He was only thinking out loud. Picturing himself flying back and forth to Austin to see Lizzie and Stella. In the past couple of days, not seeing them had become unacceptable to him.

"What?"

"I could get a place. Hell, you two could live in it. I'd have my own room and fly down at least twice a month. You could teach, have your freedom, and I'd still be around enough that she'll know me. And I'll know her."

Lizzie's pause wasn't unexpected. He was kind of taking a step back himself as he heard his own words. But when he replayed the idea it wasn't horrible.

The third time around, he was thinking about size, location, number of bedrooms—trying to get a mental image of how it would all look.

"No."

Her word cut him short right when he was starting to feel optimistic again. Turning to look at her on the bench seat beside him in the open-air train, he said, "You won't even think about it?"

"No." With the baby carrier on her lap, she looked out the window.

"Why not?"

"I'm not going to be a kept woman, Nolan. I'm not some woman you got knocked up." She spoke softly, though there was no one on the seats in front of or behind them.

The fierceness of her words cut into him.

"I didn't mean for you to get pregnant, either. I'm certain we were careful, every single time."

She glanced his way, then away, and nodded.

"And you aren't just 'some woman,' Lizzie." Not that it mattered now, any of it. She'd gotten pregnant. They had a baby. And their lives weren't destined to be lived together.

Nolan Fortune knew to stick to the facts.

"What do you want from me?" he finally asked.

"For you to let me live my life with Stella, just as I planned."

We don't need you. He heard the words she didn't say.

"Two weekends a month is all I'm suggesting," he said. "They can be like this, like today. Or you can take time to do things on your own, for yourself, while I spend time with Stella."

Visitation. That's what he'd managed to come up with. A concept as old as divorce.

"You suggested that I live in your place."

Okay, so she didn't like the idea of him buying a place for them. She hadn't objected to the visitation. To seeing him twice a month. That was the biggie. Humming with anticipation, he could hardly sit still. He focused on the green-and-yellow blanket draped over the top handle of the carrier, protecting his daughter from the air blowing in on them from outside the slow-moving train.

"I was just being practical," he tried to assure her. "It's cheaper for me to invest in real estate than to rent and the place would be vacant most of the time. I intend to pay support for Stella, and was thinking I could do so with the same money I was spending on my own visits." He'd been thinking like the money man he was, if he'd been thinking at all. He'd thrown the idea out as soon as it occurred to him.

"It would make sense, too, in that she wouldn't have to be shuffled between your home and wherever I'm staying every time I come see her."

He was sweating—with angst, and with sweet anticipation, too. Could he really make this work? Could it be this simple?

Lizzie wasn't immediately shaking her head or saying no, which increased his adrenaline rush.

"What's going to happen when I start dating? I'm going to bring my boyfriend into your home?"

His good mood flew out with the open air. But he quickly adjusted. Tried to see the new picture she'd presented.

"It would be your home, Lizzie," he told her. He wasn't sure exactly what he was feeling—he was still sorting things out. He only knew that he had to keep Lizzie and Stella in his life.

Chapter Twelve

Lizzie told herself not to get too excited. There was no happily-ever-after for her and Stella and Nolan. She knew that.

But if he was truly thinking about getting a place in Austin, giving up his "band time" over to "Stella time," did that mean that he was planning not to tell his family about them, ever?

Why? she wondered. Weren't they good enough?

As hurt as she was by that—for Stella's sake more than her own—she was also relieved. If he'd leave her with uncontested custody and the freedom to raise Stella full-time, she'd agree to live in a thatch hut on the prairie. Stella would have the benefit of knowing her father—of having a biological relative in the background in case something ever happened to Lizzie—and they could all just get on with their lives.

It was a near-perfect plan.

And it left her feeling...flat. Used.

Nolan Fortune—if she was truly spending time with the millionaire, not his alter ego—had spent the past couple of days showing her he was a good man. Aware. Considerate. Conscientious. For a guy who said he spent his days wheeling and dealing high finance, he was sure aware of the feelings of those around him. Or her feelings at least. He was doing everything he could to respect her wishes, to give her what she needed. Maybe that was what made him good at his job. It also made him a companion that hung around in your heart even after he was gone.

A companion a girl would fall in love with if she spent too much time around him.

She couldn't go that route again. She hadn't been enough for him the year before—enough to compel him to give her a way to stay in touch, or enough to be driven at least to be honest with her.

And she wasn't enough for him now, either. Stella was. And that was what she had to remember.

"Will you at least think about letting me provide a home for you and Stella here in Austin? With a room for me to stay in twice a month or so?"

She'd bet it would be nicer than a thatched hut if he was planning to stay there, too.

"Before I even agree to think about it there'd need to be some clear understandings," she said as they rounded the last corner that would take them out of the hills and onto the last long stretch through a lovely state park to the train station. Clinging to the carrier with both arms, she told herself she had no reason to feel so alone. So insecure.

She was Stella's mother. Nolan was respecting her position completely, letting her set their pace, their boundaries. She was hogging the baby. She knew that. He'd rubbed Stella's back a time or two more when Lizzie had been holding her, but that was all. It was wrong, the way she was hoarding their daughter. Yet she couldn't seem to let go, even a tiny bit.

If she gave him anything, would he take it all? Including her heart again?

"You want your name on the deed?" he asked, interrupting the negative turn her thoughts had taken again. What was wrong with her? She'd always been one to see the positive side of life. To take pleasure in little things.

"Probably, yes," she said, though that thought hadn't been forefront on her mind. Did she dare tell him she wanted him to sign away all custodial rights? What if he hadn't even thought about taking them from her? Would she be borrowing trouble where there'd been none?

Putting ideas in his head that he didn't want there?

"What else?"

The station was in sight. Thank God.

"You just laid this on me, Nolan. Give me some time to process," she said, not realizing how harsh she sounded until she saw the blank look cover his face.

She'd hurt him and that was the last thing she'd meant to do.

She might wish the man hadn't come back into her life. He might have broken her heart. But he was a good man trying to do the right thing.

And she wasn't going to turn into a shrew just because life hadn't gone exactly as she'd hoped.

"I'm sorry. That wasn't… I'm just…"

She didn't get to finish the thought. He leaned over, kissed her and was facing forward so quickly again she could hardly believe it had even happened.

Based on the statuesque way he was sitting there, as

though frozen, she had a feeling his spontaneous action hadn't been in his plan, either.

It had been only a peck.

But, oh, God, she'd felt it all the way through her.

Still in shock, she handed him the baby carrier as they got off the train, and took the bags to handle herself. He'd bought enough Christmas outfits to dress Stella for a month. And toys that would overflow her bin. She was hoping to talk him into going with her to donate some of it the next day, hoping he wouldn't be offended.

Nolan Forte would have gladly complied.

When they got to the car, and Stella woke up before they could get her settled in her seat, Lizzie unhooked the baby and held Stella out to her father. It wasn't time for her to eat yet. She wasn't fussy. "You want to hold her?" she asked.

They weren't going to talk about the kiss.

Walking around to the trunk of her car, he stopped. Stared at her, and then at Stella.

Without a word he approached, his gaze only on Stella, and then he looked up at Lizzie again, as though questioning. She smiled, not on purpose, it just came, and carefully handed the baby over, her forearm resting momentarily on his. "She's pretty good with her neck and head now, but you still need to make sure you support it at all times."

She laid the baby right in the crook of his arm. He didn't move. Didn't adjust her at all. Just stood there, staring down at her, the oddest look on his face.

She'd never known an expression could show such a wealth of emotion. She'd read about it. Seen actors do it. But this was just a guy in a parking lot. Falling in love with his baby girl.

She loaded the bags in the trunk, wanting to give him time. And then took her phone out of her purse and snapped a couple of pictures. Just so there'd be something to show Stella someday, if this was the last time they ever heard from Nolan Fortune.

He didn't even seem to notice. The baby's flailing fingers had landed on his lips and he was kissing them.

Lizzie jolted, turned away, pulling her keys out of her back pocket, ready to get the baby in her seat and head home. Filled with shame, with jitters she couldn't explain, she took a couple of seconds to compose herself, hardly believing that she was jealous of her own daughter.

"You okay, man?" Daly's comment, as the band made last-minute plug-ins, checks and adjustments Wednesday night, was softly voiced, but Branham and Glenn were both looking on from their own positions on the stage.

"Great," Nolan said, shrugging in the way a cool guy did when he wanted to be left alone. "Couldn't be better."

He was fine. He dropped his plug-in, twice, and stumbled over a mic stand, sore because he'd run five miles after he'd left Lizzie and Stella that afternoon, and then skipped dinner.

"I'm good," he said, looking behind him to include Branham and Glenn in his comment. "Let's get this thing started."

So he could hit the sack and wake up ready to go in the morning.

In a completely new world. One that contained a tiny being who trusted him enough to lay securely in against his body. Who couldn't lift a finger to help herself. Who couldn't defend herself.

So tiny and fragile.

She had so much to learn, this beautiful child with Fortune blood in her veins. He had a lifetime of commitment and responsibility to plan for. A life to support and protect in ways that had nothing at all to do with finances. The Fortune money wasn't going to take care of this one.

He was.

The second he'd held that weight against him he'd known the difference between a father and a daddy, and knew which one he wanted his daughter to have.

For the next several hours he lost himself in the music. On break he drank water, had a sandwich. And by the time he finally did get to bed, he was more like his old self.

He had his everyday life with his family in New Orleans. He had his "time out," whether it was music or something else—something like Lizzie and Stella. He had it all under control.

Life was good.

He could do this.

On Thursday when Nolan texted and suggested that they spend the day at the Armadillo Christmas Bazaar, Lizzie couldn't help the feeling of excitement that swept through her.

She'd talked to Carmela the night before about Nolan's offer to buy her a place to live and while her friend didn't love the idea, thinking the arrangement would add a complication she didn't need to an eventual *real* relationship, she thought Lizzie deserved to have Nolan pay her expenses. Her friend had also been emphatic that if Lizzie took him up on his offer, she needed to be certain that her name was on the deed, and her name only. Otherwise she'd be living at his mercy—always needing to make certain that she pleased him so that he didn't take her home from her.

Of course, even with her name on the deed, he could quit paying bills whenever he chose, but in that event, she could always sell the place if she had to.

It was going to work. Had to work. Stella would have her father in her life, she'd have the backing of any security he could provide and she and Lizzie could still have their lives. The little girl would be raised with love, not money.

Lizzie would always be a bit afraid that Nolan's family could find out about them—that at any point they could wield their money and power to take Stella from her, at least part-time—but that fear was going to be a permanent part of her life now. It was something she was going to have to live with. Nolan was from an extremely wealthy family, and the fear that they might learn he had a daughter, that they might try to take control of their granddaughter, was something she'd learn to manage.

And if the whole thing left her woman's heart a bit… bereft…then that was something she'd learn to manage, too.

Nolan had offered them a way to make this work, and she had to give everything she had to make that happen.

He'd wanted her rules, her guidelines, her conditions…whatever. She had a few days to come up with specifics.

In the meantime, she had to show him that they could do this.

With that thought in mind, she chose one of the

Christmas outfits Nolan had purchased the day before and dressed the baby, complete with a red headband and red silk bow with green holly leaves, so that they could take pictures with Santa at the Armadillo Christmas Bazaar.

Carmela was studying from home that day—working on her senior project during her holiday break from school—and she and Nolan managed civil hellos when he arrived.

He'd rented a luxurious SUV, Lizzie found as she followed him out to the parking lot.

"Do you mind if I keep it here?" he asked her as he helped her move the car seat base from her car to the rental. "We can stop in at the agency and give them your driver's license to have you added as a driver," he told her. And then added, "I just can't have the band seeing it."

Because they didn't know who he was.

And if they knew, and knew she had a kid, his family could find out.

"Of course," she told him.

Was he going to rent a car every time he came to town? Or buy one and keep it at her house?

So many things to figure out.

There was no reason for her to feel embarrassed, or like she wasn't good enough, because he hadn't been willing to spend the next week riding around in her car.

It had been fine the year before.

"I can drive my own car," she said, telling herself he hadn't meant any harm. That he was just being himself, which was what she'd wanted. That she was going to have to get used to their differences, to not take offense every time her lifestyle didn't live up to his expectations. She couldn't spend the rest of her life feeling like she wasn't enough. "I don't need to be an added driver to this one," she added, just to clarify. She didn't even want to drive it. The thing had to be worth sixty thousand dollars or more. She'd be too nervous behind the wheel. What if she wrecked it? Or someone slammed into her?

She'd just strapped herself in as she said it, glanced back at Stella in the rearview mirror attached to her carrier, who was freshly fed and wide awake in the backseat, directly behind Nolan, and tried to pretend that she wasn't hurt.

And that she wasn't worried that her daughter would barf up her breakfast all over the expensive leather interior. She'd gotten a couple of good burps out of her, but you never knew...

"I just thought... No, you're right," he said before letting her know what he thought, and she found herself desperately wanting to know. Good or bad. Who was this man?

How much of Forte had been real?

"I wanted to drive," he told her then. "It didn't feel right to ask to take over your car. To use your gas. And... I'll just buy another car seat. I'm going to need one, anyway."

He'd been thinking of her? About the hassle of switching the base back and forth? She'd have expected Nolan Forte to be as thoughtful...so why not Nolan Fortune?

Surely she wasn't guilty of some kind of reverse discrimination. Moneyed people, in spite of their power, could also be kind. Thoughtful. Unselfish.

Ashamed of herself, she smiled at him, told him she was scared to death to drive such an expensive vehicle, and when he assured her she'd be fine, and that she'd be fully insured, she agreed to have her name added to the lease as a driver.

* * *

Lizzie found herself wanting to agree with pretty much everything Nolan suggested as they made their way through the bazaar. Stella slept through parts of it, but when she was awake, her eyes were wide open as she studied the twinkling lights lining the booths, the colorful wares on display. It turned out that there was no Santa for her to have her picture taken with after all, but it wasn't like she'd have understood the significance of the jolly old man at her age. The place was overflowing with unique art, glasswork, paintings and jewelry, woodworking, spices and window frames with pressed flowers in the glass. Nolan offered to buy everything she stopped to look at, and while she couldn't let herself give in to him—she had no need for the things and nowhere to store them—after a while she was pretty sure he was just messing with her. His teasing tone made her laugh out loud. She gave him a playful shove, and almost melted when his warm grin washed over her.

"I just want you to have everything your heart desires," he said softly, his gaze completely serious all of a sudden.

Even if her heart desired him?

"I have what my heart desires," she said, meaning Stella, but unable to pull her gaze away from his.

He swallowed, his jaw tensing as his eyes filled with deep emotion. She thought he was going to say more, but he looked ahead, breaking the trance that had been holding her hostage, and she could breathe again.

Standing outside a public restroom after lunch, waiting for Lizzie to feed Stella, Nolan people-watched. The indoor bazaar was bustling with rows of booths and shopping extravaganzas. He'd been trying like hell not to do something stupid—like calling his parents and telling them that he was a father—when his phone buzzed a text message.

You need to play for the Christmas Eve party. Mom's stressing out about you being gone again. Text and tell her you'll play...

His oldest sister, Georgia, was bossing him around as usual. Which snapped his head on straight. There was no way he could tell his folks about Stella. Not yet. Because he'd told Lizzie he wouldn't, of course.

But also because he needed time to prepare them.

A plan to prepare them.

Skipping Christmas again would not prepare them for anything good.

He only had seven more days with Lizzie. Christmas Eve and Christmas Day, Tuesday and Wednesday of the following week, would only leave him five.

It was Stella's first Christmas. He wanted every second he could squeeze with Lizzie, too. Carmela was staying in town this year, but Lizzie had given him the full ten days, which meant that he could spend the entire day with them.

And he had to think of the future. The big picture. His family eventually accepting, welcoming, his illegitimate child, made with a woman he'd only known for two weeks.

He wasn't a kid. Couldn't live in the moment anymore.

Scrolling down to a different text conversation, one between him and his mother, he responded to her request of two days before to play a set of holiday carols at the annual Fortune Christmas Eve party.

Yes.

Perversely he didn't respond to Georgia.
Nor did he want to tell Lizzie what he'd done.

Chapter Thirteen

Lizzie saw Nolan texting when she came out of the bathroom. And just like that reality hit. Like the year before, she could kid herself that living in the moment was the right choice. That any moments with him were better than none. Why her heart was so glued to Nolan she had no idea, but she couldn't deny that the man brought a depth to her life, an excitement, that no one else did.

Not even Stella—not in the same way. Stella was a part of her, one that would eventually leave her to have a life of her own. Nolan… He seemed like a part of her that was going to be right there beside her until the day she died. Stella was a blessing. Nolan was a partner.

Except…no. He wasn't.

When Nolan was in Texas he had no responsibilities other than showing up to play the sax every night. He was the one who said so. These two weeks every year were his time away from responsibility.

But he had an entire life filled with high-pressured responsibilities.

People who had the right and privilege of texting him anytime they might feel the need.

People to whom he'd respond.

He was using his expensive cell phone, not the cheaper version she'd seen the year before. Presumably the one she'd seen had been the one he mentioned purchasing only for band use. The number he'd given her. The reminder that she hadn't warranted access to the Fortune number hurt all over again.

And then she reminded herself that he'd given her that number this time around, even before he'd known about Stella.

Still, to see him on that phone, attached to his real life…

For all she knew, he could already have a team of lawyers representing his family in terms of Stella. She'd believed in him once, with her whole heart, and he'd been hiding the truth from her the entire time. She'd had absolutely no idea. Would have bet her life on him.

And she'd have lost.

He looked up and saw her, and Lizzie tried to appear as though she was just exiting the restroom. She also tried to forget the glow in his eyes, the warmth in his smile, tried not to feel her own intense response to him, as he rejoined them.

He was Nolan Fortune and she could not afford to forget that.

The bazaar was known for its live entertainment, featuring a mixture of local talent and Grammy Award winners on an intimate stage—one of the reasons Nolan had chosen the destination for their day's activity, because he and Lizzie were both musicians. The first band was onstage within minutes from Lizzie feeding Stella after lunch.

The act was local—a country music trio with violin, guitar and bass—and their Texas rendition of traditional Christmas carols, while different, was quite good. Stella, who'd been asleep when Lizzie came out of the restroom, woke up when the music started, fussing, and when Nolan bent to get her out of her stroller, Lizzie picked her up immediately, bouncing gently to the beat of the music as she sang words to the instrumental entertainment.

He couldn't really hear her voice, except for a note or two now and then, but strained to catch as much as he could. Though he'd asked several times the year before, she'd never sung for him, but he knew she used to sing in choirs and was certified to teach vocal as well as instrumental music.

He'd suggested once that she do a number or two with the band, adding vocals to their jazz, but she'd pulled back immediately, telling him that she preferred her music engagement to be from the sidelines. She didn't want the limelight.

Another reason she'd never fit into his real lifestyle. In New Orleans, the Fortunes were recognized pretty much everywhere they went.

Which was why he never played in clubs there.

The trio segued from one song to the next and broke into a lively rendition of "Santa Claus Is Coming to Town." A few shoppers started to dance in the aisles and, without thinking, Nolan put his arm around Lizzie as she held Stella on her hip, encompassing both of them, and then, with his other hand on her opposite shoulder, guided them into a country-western two-step.

Laughing up at him, Lizzie fell into step, her body moving with his, their hips in contact again and again.

A mating ritual.

People were watching them. He caught them out of the corner of his eye. Used to attention, and the attention Stella was getting by looking too adorable in her little red tights and holly Christmas dress and bow, he felt a surge of adrenaline like he hadn't felt in…a year.

"You're good at this," he said, looking down at Lizzie as he continued to move them in beat to the music. "Why haven't we done this before?"

Her smile faded as she met his gaze. She didn't miss a step, but the moment changed. "We were busy doing other things," she told him.

Her lips were right there, lifted up to him, no longer talking, and he was lowering his head to them before he realized it.

Stella, whose arms and legs had been haphazardly flinging as he'd learned was normal for babies of that age, kneed him in the rib. It didn't hurt. Barely touched him, really, but the little love tap reminded him why he was there. Who he was.

And who he wasn't.

They were late getting back on Thursday and Nolan had to take off as soon as he parked the SUV in her lot. She'd offered to drop him off at his hotel, but he hadn't wanted to take any chances on being seen by his band members. She was at the passenger car door, directly behind his driver's door, unbuckling Stella's removable carrier, when he handed her the keys.

Turning, she took them, and then froze as he leaned in, kissed her cheek, gave Stella's foot a gentle little tug and left without another word.

She watched his back until he disappeared from sight.

Inside, she saw a note from Carmela telling her that her friend was at the library for the evening.

She bathed Stella, dressed her in a gray onesie with white hearts and pink trim around the neck and long sleeves, and an hour later was still shaking inside.

Putting Stella in her swing, she picked up her phone, searched the new contact for Nolan Fortune and pushed to text.

We need to talk.

She could picture him, standing in his hotel room—she'd only allow him still dressed in the day's black jeans and red button-down shirt, not going into or coming from the shower—phone in hand, reading her text.

Could she do it? Could she be his secret?

Have bimonthly visits from a man who lived a life she knew very little about?

She could look up the New Orleans Fortunes on the internet. But Lizzie hadn't wanted to become an internet stalker. Hadn't wanted to see Nolan's life laid bare before her on-screen.

Couldn't bear to open that door.

As long as there was a possibility that she could raise Stella outside of the hoopla, the privileged environment, she would fight to do so.

She just wanted Stella to know how it felt to be an average person before she was consumed by the elite and powerful.

Her phone vibrated in her hand.

Tonight after the last set? If you call at midnight, I'll pick up.

The first time they'd made love had been on a night that had started like that—her calling him after the last set to invite him up to her place. Carmela had been gone and she'd thrown caution and all her years of introversion and conservative upbringing to the wind and invited a man she barely knew to her apartment.

But it hadn't felt like she'd barely known him. It had felt as though he'd been her soul mate.

Trembling, fighting something she knew she couldn't have, a temptation she didn't dare allow, she didn't text back.

Talking at night made sense. With Stella, and being out and about as they were when they were together during the day, there was always the chance they'd be interrupted. Besides, over the phone was much safer than in person.

She wanted to be able to just do it. To call him in the intimacy of late-night privacy, and work things out. She needed to be able to. She was just so damned scared. Out of her wits. What if she really did love him?

A ghost?

Could she live with herself if she became his occasional lover, knowing that eventually he'd marry someone else and produce legitimate heirs for his parents?

She was already behaving in ways that made her ashamed of herself. Hogging Stella as she mostly did. Grabbing the baby up before he could.

He backed away every time. Allowing her to be the boss where their daughter was concerned, which made her feel even more selfish.

Nolan was treating them like gold. Willing to provide everything and take very little. His caring ripped at the walls she'd built around her heart. A look in his eye had melted a year's worth of ice.

But how did she agree to any kind of relationship with a man she didn't trust?

Nolan broke with his general practice and had a beer during the first set. He just needed a little help to relax, to slide deeply enough into his music to give the audience what they'd come to hear.

On break, he switched to ice water. He was swabbing his horn when his phone buzzed a text, and he was on it in a heartbeat.

Thank you, son! See you soon!

His mother. Responding to his text from earlier in the day.

He opened the text from Lizzie again, checked again to see the notation that his response had been delivered…and saw nothing further from her.

We have to talk wasn't usually a good thing.

He swabbed his horn again, checked his low EB pad for moisture when his phone buzzed again.

His heart tripped a beat when he saw the new text icon on his screen.

She'd sent a picture of him holding Stella—obviously taken the day before since that was the only time he'd ever held the baby. He hadn't known she'd snapped the shot, wanted immediately to set it as his wallpaper, but he'd told her he wouldn't say anything about having a daughter.

So he spent the rest of his break looking at his phone, again and again, studying the picture of that tiny bundle in his arms, so filled with love for her he could hardly breathe, and trying to convince himself that whatever talk he and Lizzie needed to have had to be okay. He hoped to God she wasn't planning to tell him goodbye.

Lizzie tried to be asleep before midnight. Stella ate at nine and was out. She shouldn't be up again for another three hours at least. The night before she'd made it almost all night—maybe because of all the daytime stimulation she was getting.

She drank chamomile tea—her doctor had told her it was a healthy herb for both her and Stella while she was nursing. The usual calming effects were lost on her that night.

A hot bath didn't help. It just made her hotter for Nolan.

And Carmela had gone to bed early because she had to be up at six to help with some project at the architectural firm.

At a quarter past twelve, she gave up trying to fight with herself. The talk had to happen. There was no point in prolonging the inevitable. When a bandage needed to come off, it was best just to rip it quickly.

She climbed out of bed, pulled on a fleece robe over her white cotton pajama pants and short matching T-shirt, headed into the bathroom adjoining her room, turned on the fan and shut the door. No point in risking waking Stella. Dropping down to the thick, shaggy beige throw rug on the floor, she opened the text message she'd sent to Nolan and hit Call.

"I'm just heading out of the club," he told her, picking up on the first ring.

At least he wasn't already back at the hotel—in bed, which was what she'd feared if she'd put off the call too long.

Picturing him dressed in the jeans and black T-shirt

and leather vest he wore to play, walking down a street filled with bars and partyers, was much better on her brain.

"First, I'm sorry I'm being so possessive where Stella is concerned," she said, getting the words out almost exactly how they'd been rehearsed. "No matter what, she's your daughter, too, and if you want to hold her, you have every right to do so."

"I'm barging in after the fact, Liz. You've done all the work, have the routine. You're the one who takes care of her. It's your say."

He was too damned understanding. Too nice. And if that was the father Stella knew, if, during their times together, whenever he could make it to Austin, this was the only side she ever knew of him, would that be so bad?

"Is Carmela home?" he asked when she just sat there, wishing she knew what to do.

"Yes." That one was easy. She had her protection right there in the next room. No way he could come up and climb into her bed with her.

"Good. Then can you come down? I'm outside."

He'd walked to her place rather than his hotel? Trembling overtook her again.

"You said we need to talk. Obviously not about the weather. I figure it's best if we do it face-to-face. No more secrets."

He had a point. But she wasn't dressed and Carmela had to be up early.

Even as she was rounding up her defenses, Lizzie was in her room, checking on the baby, who was sound asleep.

"Okay," she said softly. "Give me a few minutes."

Hanging up, she pulled on orange sweats, a T-shirt

and a dark blue hoodie, which she zipped almost to the chin. She stopped in Carmela's room, just letting her friend know she was stepping outside to talk to Nolan for a few, and when Carmela sat up, she pushed her friend gently by the shoulder. "Go back to sleep," she said. "I just wanted you to know I'm not here in case Stella cries. But I'm taking the monitor with me."

She wasn't going anywhere with him. And the talk wasn't going to take long.

"Be careful, Liz."

"Always."

Carmela's worried glance followed her to the door.

Chapter Fourteen

Watching as Lizzie walked out toward the parking lot where he waited for her, he was reminded of the few mornings last year he'd been lucky enough to wake up next to her. He wanted to kiss her. To take her in his arms, hold her tight and not let go.

"Hey," she said, walking with him to a pony wall that separated a grassy area from the sidewalk.

"Hey." He sat with her, his shoulder touching hers purposefully. She scooted down, clearly stating her purpose.

In his short-sleeved black T-shirt, with the jeans and black boots, he could have fit into any bar in the area. His family wouldn't recognize him.

"You asked me what my parameters would be if you were to buy a place here and I were to live in it with Stella."

Thank God. She wasn't saying goodbye. That in itself was a relief. "Absolutely. Tell me what you need."

Back in New Orleans, he knew how to keep business partners happy. To keep his family happy. This moment felt more important than either of those.

"First, my name and only my name would have to be on the deed."

He'd planned on both their names. But he wanted her happy. "Done."

"I choose the place. I won't live in some fancy neighborhood where I constantly feel out of place. Where my car will stick out and people will raise their eyebrows."

He'd have liked to have her in an upscale house in a part of town where she'd be looked after in his absence.

"As long as it's safe, with safe neighborhoods all around, fine."

His negotiating skills, usually a strongpoint, sucked.

"When you're in town, using the house, you'll have to let me know your schedule. No just popping in and out unannounced."

She was seriously considering his offer. He held back a grin. "Fine."

"You'd have your own set of rooms, and be responsible for keeping them clean."

He'd figured he'd be hiring a housekeeper, but chose to keep that conversation for another time.

"Yep."

Relief was almost as much of a high as sitting there with the woman in his dreams, knowing that they had a child together.

They could spend the rest of his time in town looking at places. Or at least as long as it took to have an accepted contract on one. He wanted it done before his ten days with her were through. To know they were settled and safe. To know he could see them every possible chance he got. He wanted to have a place to come home to twice in January.

Resisting the urge to take her hand, to kiss the palm, and then the rest of her, he shoved his fingers under his thighs, trapping them against hard, cold cement.

"There will be no physical relationship between us of any kind."

Breath seeped out of him at her words. He couldn't speak until he took a moment to let his lungs refill.

He had to be honest with her about what he wanted— what he hoped for between them. He was pretty sure he'd used up his allotment of lying to her for the rest of their lives.

"Can I just add a caveat that if at any time in the future things change with our situation and we are both fully consenting, we can reopen the physical relationship dialogue?"

"I'm not going to change, Nolan."

"I'm not saying you are." He glanced over at her, unable to make out her expression with her long hair falling on either side of her face. "I told you I would be completely honest with you. And, in all honesty, I'm finding you every bit as irresistible now as I ever did." He felt her stiffen, and back-pedaled. "I'm not saying I want to have sex with you," he added. "I agree one hundred percent that it would be a stupid idea at this point in our lives. But I need you to know that the feelings I had for you last year, sexual and otherwise… they're still here."

Taking a deep breath when he feared that he'd scared her off, he added, "I'm just saying that if, sometime in the future, something changes, I might want to mention it to you."

"I can't have you in my home, staying there, with this…this…possibility…hanging there between us."

He understood. Totally. Wished he didn't.

"I know."

"So you agree. No possibility of sex."

"I agree because I also want what's best for our daughter."

Pressing his fingers against the wall beneath him, he waited in the darkness. It was cool out. Low sixties, maybe colder. He shouldn't be sweating.

"Okay. As long as you agree to leave if things get out of hand, if I start to feel uncomfortable with you there. You know, sexually. Like pressured or something."

Okay!

He brushed off the agreeing-to-leave part. He'd do it. He just didn't have to linger on the idea.

She might date someday. Even as quiet and shy as she was, her beauty couldn't help but attract male attention. Once Stella was a little older and…

He shut the door on those thoughts. No sense borrowing trouble.

He was going to get her to agree to letting him buy her a house—one that would be a home to him, too, twice a month or so, when he came to visit his daughter and the mother of his child. At the moment he couldn't imagine a better gift.

She wouldn't have to work so hard. And she'd be able to spend as much time with Stella as she wanted, could enjoy life more than she'd ever been able to do before.

She didn't trust him. He got that.

But he was still in love with her. He got that, too. And a part of him believed she still had feelings for him.

Their arrangement wasn't typical. Probably wouldn't work for a lot of people. But this was him and Lizzie. A fantasy that had become reality.

Chapter Fifteen

Carmela was up and waiting for Lizzie when she came back inside half an hour later.

She didn't bother to ask her friend, who was in fleece Christmas tree pajama pants and a matching red top sitting up with a cup of tea on the couch, why she was still awake.

"You should be in bed," she said instead. "You have to be up early."

"You think I was going to sleep lying in there?" Carmela shot back, giving Lizzie the once-over about half a dozen times. If ever there was a protective bear, Carmela was it, and Lizzie loved her for it.

Just as she knew she could never allow herself to need it. Carmela would be graduating and getting on with her life soon. She'd need to be able to leave Lizzie and Stella behind without guilt.

"I agreed to it," she said, figuring that the sooner

they got through the conversation, the sooner her friend would get the rest she needed.

"What did he agree to?" They'd talked it all over the night before. Over and over. And again that morning before Carmela had left, and more that evening, too, when her friend finally got home.

"All of it," she said, shrugging as she dropped down into an armchair, her feet up in it with her.

"He agreed to give you the full deed to the house?" Carmela's eyes wide, she held her teacup halfway to her mouth.

"You didn't expect him to?"

"I guess I did." Carmela broke eye contact, but only for a second. "I just… I don't know, maybe I hoped…"

"What?"

No answer came to mind.

"I think I hoped he'd ask you to marry him," Carmela said softly, standing just behind her. "Didn't you, Lizzie? Even a little bit?"

Tears sprang to her eyes, the first she'd shed all day, and Carmela wrapped her in a hug. "It's okay, sweetie. I love how you always manage to hold on to hope until the very last minute," she said, giving Lizzie one more squeeze before letting her go.

"I would have said no," Lizzie told her, sniffing as she wiped away the little bit of tears that had fallen. "There's no way he's going to give up his life, and no way I could ever fit into it. Even if he'd asked me to. But I knew he wouldn't. Not with what happened with his former girlfriend." She'd told Carmela about Molly. And about Nolan's older brother, too, who'd married a woman after only knowing her two weeks.

The Fortune family had survived it all just fine, but that didn't take the sting out of the burn.

"I guess it's good that he's buying you a house…"

"…and an SUV with a lifetime service agreement," Lizzie snuck in, because she wanted to give due where it was deserved. She wanted Carmela to know all of the facts because she needed her friend's opinion.

She didn't trust herself enough where Nolan was concerned to rely fully on her own.

"Wow!" Carmela said, her brow raised. And then, frowning again, she shook her head. "Still, I really didn't think he'd just walk away…"

"I'd hardly call a couple of visits a month 'walking away.'"

"Yeah and how long do you think that will last?" Carmela asked. "Until he starts seeing someone else." She glanced at Lizzie and then added, "Or you do."

She'd needed her friend's honest opinion. But that didn't mean hearing it was painless.

The microwave binged, letting Lizzie know her cup of tea was ready, and she figured there was nothing left to do but drink it, get sleepy and go to bed.

"You got pretty much everything you wanted, and then some," Carmela said as the two turned out lights and headed down the hall.

"Yep."

They stopped outside Carmela's door. "You don't seem real happy about that."

She didn't feel happy. "I think I'm just on overload," she said. "And exhausted," she added. "We're going house hunting tomorrow. I'm sure everything will start to seep in then and I'll be excited."

Reaching up, Carmela smoothed a piece of hair away from Lizzie's cheek. "Your life is going to be so much easier, sweetie."

Yeah. Monetarily. Which had never mattered all that

much to her, not that anyone else could seem to understand that.

"You still love him, don't you?"

"I hope not. Because if I do, I don't see how this is going to work."

By the time Nolan picked up Lizzie and Stella on Friday, midmorning, he already had a Realtor from Austin Elite Real Estate lining up homes for them to see.

While a part of him felt uncomfortable, buying a house without anyone in his family knowing what he was doing, he couldn't get the job done fast enough. He had his own money, could pay cash for the house, and no one would be the wiser. But his family…they told each other about major activities in their lives.

Especially since Austin's debacle. They'd all learned to make sure that the family had each other's backs.

Stella, in another of her new Christmas outfits, a red one-piece with a red, white and green netted skirt and three-dimensional holly balls on the top, had their Realtor, a middle-aged woman who'd been in the business more than twenty years, entranced. She assumed Nolan and Lizzie were a couple.

With a glance at Lizzie, who'd shrugged, he let the assumption lie untouched. Just seemed easier than trying to explain the truth of their situation.

Sandra had shown them three houses, driving ahead of them, while Nolan and Lizzie and Stella followed in the rented SUV, when Stella, who'd been sleeping on and off, started to get fussy.

They had an appointment to see the fourth house, and because it was owner-occupied it would be their only window until after the holiday. The house, a two-story with split double master suites, was at the top of his list.

"We're about fifteen minutes away," Nolan said to Lizzie. Their appointment was in thirty minutes. "I'll let Sandra know we're going to stop and will meet her there." He had all of the addresses already typed into the GPS system. And he was already asking the voice search to find the closest library. They'd have clean restrooms. But with the crying, his virtual assistant couldn't make out his request.

"It's okay," Lizzie said, raising her voice to be heard over the sound of the crying as she motioned to the parking lot of one of Austin's more impressive office buildings. "Just pull in here. I can feed her in the car."

Heart pumping for no sane reason, he did as she asked, finding a spot off in a far corner that had trees lining the spaces. She was already out of the vehicle and climbing into the backseat by the time he'd turned off the engine.

And in what seemed like only seconds, the crying had stopped, replaced by small sucking sounds. Because the car seat was right behind Nolan, Lizzie was sitting on the opposite side of the car. If he turned his head just a little bit, he could see her out of the corner of his eye.

He didn't.

But he had to fight hard not to.

Tapping his thumb on the steering wheel, he looked at the trees, started to whistle one of the newer tunes the band was doing. The radio music he'd been playing, a streaming Christmas channel, had gone off with the car.

Thinking of Lizzie breast-feeding their baby was overwhelming. It warmed him in a way he'd never experienced before.

"Does it hurt?" he finally blurted when his imagination was taking him places he didn't feel comfortable going. Not without her knowledge. "My sisters…none of them have kids yet," he added, feeling like a complete idiot. He tried to distract himself, focusing on the bug-splattered windshield. It needed to be cleaned. He'd do that the next time he gassed up.

"At first it did," she said, after long enough that he'd assumed he wasn't going to get an answer, and was already formulating an apology for crossing one of the many unseen lines they seemed to have drawn between them.

All necessary lines.

"Or rather, after the first day or so. At first, it was really cool. Indescribable. Then my nipples got raw and so sore it was excruciating."

"Is that normal?" he asked.

"Yep. They give you lotion, but mostly you just have to get through the toughening-up part, and then it's great again."

Stella's breathing was heavier as she sucked and swallowed. It took upon a rhythm. *Shhhhd, gull, shhhhd, gull.* And then faster, as though she couldn't get enough. *Shhhhd, gull, shhhhd, gull.* And slowing again.

He played around in his head with attaching different notes to them. Had a thought about writing a piece. A mother's love song. His love song to the mother of his child. Would she accept it?

Thankfully, he was smart enough not to ask *that* question.

Lizzie managed to keep herself emotionally distanced on Friday as they looked at homes. The last appointment ran late and she and Nolan only had a few minutes to talk on the way home.

"So which house was your favorite today?"

She knew his. The fourth one. He'd told her so while they were in it, and twice afterward, too.

"Honestly?" Stella was sleeping in her car seat and Lizzie really just wanted to lie down and join her.

"Of course."

"I didn't like any of them," she said. If this was going to work, she had to speak up. "I mean, they were beautiful homes, but I didn't feel comfortable in them. At home in them. I felt like a visitor from the wrong side of the tracks."

That wasn't completely accurate, either. But it was as close as she could get to explaining the tightness in her chest, the desire to leave, that she'd experienced in every home they'd toured.

"I'm sorry." She prepared herself for his frustration. Disappointment. Things she'd not really experienced the year before.

Because their relationship hadn't been real. They'd had no opportunity to experience differences of opinion, hardship or challenges.

She had no idea how Nolan handled any of the above, except to know that, in the end, he'd bailed.

And yet, she wanted to know that part of him. If they were going to coparent, live in the same home when he was in town, they were going to have to leave the fairy tale of last year behind and learn how to have a real relationship. One where they actually did disagree about things.

Truth was, she wanted that relationship. Badly. Wanted to know the whole Nolan, not just his fantasy parts.

"Was there anything you liked about any of them?" he asked, sounding more like Sandra than someone with an actual stake in which house they chose.

"Of course!" She went on to list at least a dozen. The landscaping in one of the yards had been a particular standout. She'd loved the water feature. And the six-foot wooden fencing. There'd been the cupboard arrangement in one of the kitchens. The carpeted bedrooms in another. They'd all had garden tubs in the master and she'd been a fan. A walk-in closet had caught her attention.

He nodded, glancing over at her as though he was fully engaged in what she was saying, but gave no opinions of his own. Maybe that was okay. This was going to be her home. A visitation spot for him.

"What did you like about that fourth house so much?" she asked. He'd pointed out the extra room that could be a playroom. The island in the kitchen for her to have room for baking.

She'd told him, the year before, that she loved to bake and had been wondering if he remembered that, or if he'd just been making assumptions.

"I liked that it had split masters," he told her. "I'd have my own area. We could even add an outside entrance. You could keep it locked off when I'm not there and not feel as though parts of your house were inaccessible to you. It'd be just off there by itself."

Okay. She hadn't thought of that. She had been trying hard all day to picture only herself and Stella in the homes. As for Nolan being there…well, she'd find a way to deal with that when the time came. Find a way not to notice how good he smelled. Or how much even the sight of his hands could make her remember them all over her.

"It was just so…big," she told him. "I was kind of thinking one-story. That ranch-style Sandra talked about. I wonder if there are any smaller homes with split masters?"

She'd never looked at homes before. Hadn't lived in a house since her parents had been killed when she was eleven.

He nodded. "I'll have Sandra type in all of your parameters for tomorrow."

They'd already agreed they'd start looking again at ten the next day.

Because they were running late, once again, Nolan had to head out the second they pulled in the lot of her apartment complex. The only thing different on Friday's departure was that he leaned into the backseat to kiss Stella before he left, telling her that Daddy loved her.

Good thing he didn't hang around long enough to see the tears that pooled in Lizzie's eyes at the sound of his voice saying those words.

He'd never told her he loved *her*. Not even during their last, intense hours of sex the night before he'd left town.

She'd never told him, either.

You still love him, don't you?

Carmela's words from the night before came back to her as she unstrapped Stella's carrier, threw the diaper bag and her purse over her shoulder and headed into the apartment.

How could she love a man she didn't really know? One she couldn't trust?

He'd bailed on her before. He could again. She just had to hope it would work out.

Somehow.

Chapter Sixteen

Stella was wide awake when they arrived at the first house on Sandra's list on Saturday, so Nolan, taking Lizzie at her word, picked the baby up.

"I'll carry her," he announced to the woman who felt so right at his side. "That way we don't have to deal with unhooking the carrier." It wasn't much to deal with. Click and click.

Lizzie didn't smile, but she didn't argue, either, as she walked with him to the front door of a modestly sized home in the same neighborhoods they'd been in the day before. The choices were all in gated communities—one of his qualifications he'd given Sandra, and yet, to him, seemed very much mainstream middle-class.

"Wow." Lizzie's eyes were wide as soon as they stepped inside.

Instead of going off on his own, as he had in every house the day before, he stayed right by her side. Partially because he wasn't sure she'd pay attention to the house if he disappeared with the baby, but also because he was just drawn to be there.

Yesterday he'd been getting a feel for how far she'd let him go in terms of opulence. Today, he knew what she needed.

He was also getting a feel for the warmth of his little girl against his chest. How could he feel so strong and capable, and so weak at the same time?

What were these Sullivan females doing to him?

"I love it out here," Lizzie said when she walked through French doors off the eating area into a backyard that, while not huge, was completely fenced and private, and had a filtered and treated waterfall and cement-bottom pond in the center of it, surrounded by flowering plants.

You'd think he'd taken her to the Taj Mahal, the way she was awed, and he wanted to take her into his arms, too. To kiss her. And laugh out loud for no reason whatsoever.

It wasn't a home he'd have chosen. There wasn't a closet in it big enough to contain all of his suits and business shoes, let alone anything else. There was no place for his cars. His art. His pool table. No place to host clients for a quiet evening at home.

But the house wasn't for him.

When Lizzie told him that she didn't need to see any more houses, that she'd made her choice, he made a full-price cash offer on the spot.

There'd still be a bit of waiting period, for a title search and paperwork, but if all went as planned, he could get Lizzie moved in the weekend between Christmas and New Year's and still make it home in time for the big Fortune New Year's bash.

Even if the papers weren't finalized yet, since the house was vacant, he could rent the place for her until closing.

Everything was going exactly as planned.

So why did he feel like he was walking a tightrope over a canyon? And yet, even feeling that way he knew there was no way he'd opt out.

He and Lizzie and Stella weren't going to be a traditional family, or even a real family at all, but they were finding a way to make "them" work. As best as they could. He told himself he was good with the arrangement.

And he hated that he'd just purchased a home for a captivating woman to live in with his child and there was no way he'd ever fit in it with them.

Saturday night, when Carmela offered to stay with Stella and strongly suggested that Lizzie head to the club to hear Nolan play, she wanted to say no. Unequivocally. To her, it felt like the wrong thing to do.

And yet, there she was, in her newest pair of jeans with a black button-down blouse that gathered at the back, black boots and the red quilted zipper vest Aunt Betty had sent her for Christmas, getting ready to pull open the door.

Her hair was down, as usual, but she'd put on full makeup for the first time since Stella was born—which for her meant foundation, blush *and* eyeliner. Most times lately it was just foundation. And, if she wanted to be fancy, a bit of blush.

Would he think she was inviting more than she was? Coming on to him?

Backing away, she leaned against the outside wall for a minute, trying not to panic.

What was she doing?

The door opened and she could hear music coming from inside. Truthfully, she missed the fact that Nolan hadn't talked to her about his music much at all. The year before, they'd talked about every song in every set. And had both been engrossed in the conversation. That in itself had set him apart for her.

This year they were taking care of their baby and buying a house.

And hardly talking to each other, about each other, at all.

Showing up at the club wasn't going to change that.

Why had Carmela started this?

She should never have come.

The door opened again, someone else going in. If she didn't hurry, there wouldn't even be seats left in the back.

A sax solo started and she stood up straight, moved forward to hear it better. Almost like she was in a trance, she continued toward that sound of the music. Nolan might not be exactly who she thought he was, but his music still called to her. It had been what had first drawn her to him the year before.

That's why she was there.

She couldn't afford fantasy. Romance. Believing in happily-ever-after or soul mates or undying love. She had to stay firmly in reality.

But Nolan's music—it was real.

And if she was going to know the real him, or find the courage to live her foreseeable future as she'd promised him she would, she couldn't leave the music out.

There was too much danger that it would creep up on her later, play with her emotions, and she'd get hurt.

Or worse, Stella would.

* * *

Nolan was just finishing the last phrase of his solo in one of the new pieces when he opened his eyes to see Lizzie standing in the doorway of the club.

Heart in his throat, he cut the last notes short and hardly noticed when the next number started without him. Was something wrong? Where was Stella?

Getting ready to put his horn down and hurry off-stage to meet her, he just stood there, looking like an imbecile, he figured, while she scoped out a table in the back and took a seat. When he noticed her speak to a waitress who approached, and saw a little white napkin placed on the table in front of her, he sent an apologetic glance to Daly and jumped into the song.

Before they'd finished another stanza Daly and Branham had both noticed Lizzie, and were grinning at him.

Guess they knew now where he'd been spending his days. They probably figured he'd hooked up with Lizzie again, as he had the year before. He was going to have to let them think it. Taking their razzing was better than getting anywhere near close to his truth.

They'd hear that soon enough. When he told them why he was quitting the band. His free time was all going to be spent in Austin now.

A tall glass of clear liquid with a straw landed on Lizzie's table. Probably the lemon-lime soda she'd had a few times when they'd been out this past week. She steered clear of caffeine and alcohol. She was nursing.

His baby.

She hadn't been drinking much the year before, either. Lizzie wasn't much of a partyer. He knew that about her.

And other things.

Like the fact that she wasn't swayed by notoriety, or money. To earn her regard you had only to be a decent person. Kind.

And honest.

He hadn't told her yet that he was going back to New Orleans for Christmas. Or that he'd been thinking more and more about telling his family about Stella while he was there.

She was not only his daughter, she was their family, too, the first Fortune grandchild, whether they liked it or not. Approved or not.

He made it through one song without goofing. And another. He didn't know how, as he was filled with a hot need to get out to Lizzie. To spend even ten minutes with her like they had the year before. Just talking about music and the way it infiltrated so many aspects of life. It was the background, the foreground, the dressing, the peace. They'd decided that.

It was the bells of heaven, Lizzie had said.

And the crescendo of perfect sex, he'd added, to which she'd eagerly agreed, climbing on top of him to ask for more.

They'd bought a house. Were starting a life together—albeit a part-time one, without an actual relationship. For Stella—not for them. Was tonight's visit her way of opening the door to more?

Could he even do that? Well, physically, damn straight he could. Right that second. But that would be making her little more than his kept woman.

Closing his eyes, he put every ounce of frustration, of denial, of want and need, into the last stanza of the last number of the set. In a few more seconds he could talk to her.

And everything would fall into place again.

A few more seconds…

He got through the note. Opened his eyes.

And Lizzie was gone.

She wasn't even in the SUV yet when her phone rang. Nolan.

She didn't want to answer. But if she didn't he might think something happened to her—a woman alone in a club at night…

"Hello."

"Where are you?"

"On my way home."

"You're walking alone?" He sounded out of breath, like he was walking fast. She unlocked his rental and got in, shutting the door, too late realizing he'd hear it shut.

"No, I'm in the SUV."

"You're still in the parking lot."

"Yes." She started the engine.

"Hold on, I'm coming out."

"No, Nolan. You have another set to do. And I have to get home." They had to be honest with each other, so she said, "Or rather, I just need to get away from you at the moment."

She put the SUV in Reverse, backing out of the parking space.

"Listening to you play, it started things all over again," she said. "Last year…the way your music sucked me in. How great it felt, how good we were together. The secret hopes and dreams that had been building in me. I can't afford to let them come back…"

Back then, she'd actually thought they might be destined to become a family.

Now she knew better.

Hell, she didn't even exist in his real life.

That apparently didn't stop her from loving him.

She had no idea what to do with that.

Nolan made it to the parking lot in time to see Lizzie pulling out of the lot. "It was great, seeing you out there, Lizzie," he told her as he watched her taillights disappear down the road. "I'm not always great at talking about what I'm feeling, but…"

"The song…the solo…it's one I hadn't heard."

"It's new this year." And he thought of her every time he played the evocative notes.

"It's good." She mentioned a couple of particular phrases, the mezzo piano into mezzo forte.

"That's it," she said then as he stood in the parking lot alone. "Forte. That's why you chose that name."

Of course she'd get that.

"I'm glad you came," he told her. "And I wish you'd stayed."

"What do you think would happen if I did?"

In a perfect world, they'd end up together again. In bed. Holding each other. Making love until dawn.

"And then what would happen in the morning?" she asked softly, letting him know her mind was filled with the same memories as his. "Or tomorrow morning? Or the end of next week?" she asked. "I'd want more, Nolan."

And so would he.

"I'm home. I have to go," she said, but didn't immediately hang up. So he did.

He let her go.

Because he was always going to have to let her go. It wasn't just the responsible thing to do, it was the kind thing to do. Lizzie was accepting his place in her life because she was a great mother. A great human being. She was sharing their daughter with him.

He could be Nolan Fortune, be a father. But he couldn't have it all.

On Sunday, Nolan suggested he and Lizzie go shopping for furniture. She was going to pick out whatever she wanted and he was going to foot the bill. The only choice he was going to make was for his own bedroom suite. The rest would be hers.

They had lunch at a pita bar, with her poring over furniture pamphlets as though her life depended on it.

Carmela was gone when they got back to the apartment, with a couple of hours before Nolan had to leave. He'd suggested taking the baby to the mall for pictures with Santa. Lizzie told him Carmela wanted to be there for that. He'd let that go, too.

"She's soaked!" Lizzie, in jeans and a long-sleeved black T-shirt with a Christmas tree on the front, was lifting the baby out of her carrier. Glancing over at Nolan, she asked, "You want to change her?"

He did. But…

"I've never changed a baby in my life." He was following her down the hall to her room, though, where, she'd told him during their shopping expedition, she had a changing table. He'd been asking about furnishings for Stella's room at the time. She'd told him she wanted a crib to match the table she already had.

Laying down Stella, who was wide awake, arms and legs moving in their random way, on the changing table, Lizzie turned to him. "You up for this?"

"Of course!" He'd been in the room before, but somehow this time, seeing the walls crowded with baby things, was a shock. Her life had truly done a one-

hundred-and-eighty-degree turn. He'd known, but in
that room, it really hit him. Wiping his mind of anything but the moment, he stepped up so close to her
their arms were touching, so that he was near enough
to tend to his daughter.

"Unsnap her here," she said as she pointed to a se-
ries of snaps running up one leg and down the other. He
did as she said, working his fingers gently from snap
to snap, undoing each one up her left leg, happy with
his ability to reach success even with her flailing legs.

"If you take that long, she's going to lose patience
with you," Lizzie said. "You've got to be quick, or play
with her to distract her attention, or she's going to get
mad." As she spoke she pulled the snaps on the other
leg apart with one quick jerk. She pointed to the diapers
tucked into a cubby on the top of the table.

"She doesn't like the cold air on her so I always grab
the new one first, have it open and ready to slip under
her before I unfasten."

Conscious of time, he grabbed quickly for the clean
diaper but ended up with two. He dropped one, opened
the other and put it on the table.

"Spread the sides open, too," Lizzie said, her fingers touching his as she showed him what she meant.

"Now, pull these tabs..." She pulled one, paused, and
he jumped in and did the other. He tried to focus. He
did not want to make his daughter angry.

"Here's the tricky part," Lizzie said, glancing over
her shoulder at him. "I'll do it this time, you get the
next..."

With a couple of quick flips and a grab, she had
Stella's tiny ankles between a couple of her fingers, the
baby's butt up in the air, soiled diaper gone and new diaper slid into place. All within about two seconds. She

took another couple of seconds to wipe the baby down with a cloth she'd grabbed from a dispenser by the diapers, and then the front of the diaper went up in place.

"You want to do that quick—"

"I know, so she doesn't get mad," he said, reaching over to pull the second tab and attach it into place when she didn't follow the first one up.

"And so she doesn't pee on you," Lizzie said, grinning at him. Her lips were so close, her beautiful brown eyes glowing and meeting his.

"A...huh." The tiny sound wasn't a wail. But it was a warning he'd already grown to recognize.

"It's okay, baby girl, Mommy's right here." Lizzie's attention was instantly fully back on the baby. "Just be patient a little bit longer while Daddy gets you snapped up," she said in the higher tone she often used with Stella. And then, while Nolan's heart tripped over and skipped beats, Lizzie entertained the baby, poking her belly and making faces and sounds, as he worked one snap at a time on the baby's bottom half.

Daddy.

Daddy!

Daddy...

Any way it sounded in his head, he wasn't ever going to be the same.

Chapter Seventeen

Nolan didn't play well Sunday night. He didn't sleep much, either. If he'd been sick, he could have taken a pill or something. His aches came from a place much deeper than bones and flesh. He was trapped between two lives that were pulling at him with equal force. Each of them filled with heart and soul, with a substance that couldn't be denied.

To be a good family member in one life meant he had to be a bad one in the other.

He'd given in to yearnings the year before, to the unreliable buzz of energy inside him, and had created a hell for himself. He saw no way out.

He and Lizzie and Carmela were supposed to take Stella to get her Christmas pictures with Santa that day before having lunch together—the four of them. His request. Carmela was family to Lizzie and Stella, not biologically, but in any way that counted to Lizzie.

Nolan thought it important that he and Carmela find a way to be comfortable around each other, too.

How could he expect the woman who seemed to see only the worst in him to be comfortable with him, when he couldn't find a peaceful place with himself?

They were going to get Christmas pictures and he hadn't even told Lizzie that he wouldn't be with them for Christmas yet. That he'd booked a flight for himself for the next afternoon, to have himself home in time for his parents' annual gathering. While not as big as the New Year's bash, by a whole lot, the Christmas Eve thing was far more important. It was a get-together with loved ones, trusted ones, not the showy party that included everyone the Fortunes had to invite.

He hadn't told Lizzie he was going because he still wasn't sure he was going to do so. He knew he should. He needed his family on his side, ready to accept the huge news he had to lay on them. And it wasn't like Stella would even be aware that it was any other day. His parents would probably be more hurt by his absence than Lizzie would be. And yet...

Monday morning, early, when he knew his older brother would be at work, he dialed Austin.

He'd told Lizzie he wouldn't say anything to anyone, but he needed answers and wasn't finding them on his own. He'd swear Austin to secrecy, but he had to talk to someone.

Somehow, even with the best of intentions and his eyes seemingly wide open, he'd mucked up his life.

"To what do I owe the privilege of a call from the one who has to escape us all?" Austin's voice replaced the phone ringing in Nolan's ear.

"Yeah, right, like you weren't the first one who couldn't wait for a little time away once upon a time," he said. Austin might be his unknowing mentor, the sibling he felt closest to, but the man didn't have to know that. And Nolan had ceased being intimidated by him about the time he'd started making notable amounts of money at the firm. Nolan had ceased acting intimidating long before that.

"So what's up? I've got an early meeting."

"We're on vacation," Nolan reminded him.

"Yeah, well, Brighton's in town."

He knew the guy. A foreign businessman who used their bank for his North American funds, to broker North American deals and to finance a multitude of North American businesses.

"Let me guess, you invited him," Nolan said. Austin's silence was his response, one that Nolan translated in the affirmative.

"Seriously, what's up?" Austin asked, his tone evincing true interest.

"I've mucked up," Nolan said. "Take your worst moment, double it and I'm there."

"You got married? What the hell? When?" The alarm coming over the phone shot straight through Nolan, mincing with his own. Compounding his own. In dark dress pants and white business shirt, minus the red tie he'd planned to wear to the mall, he paced his hotel room. Irritated by the brushing sound his stocking feet made against the carpet, he'd never felt weaker in his life.

He should have put on his new wingtips before he made the call.

"I'm not married," he said. "I knew better than that." No, what he'd done was far worse. "I need you to swear that you'll keep this to yourself. Give me time to figure out what I'm going to do. And then let me tell Dad myself."

"Are you in jail? Or in danger of going there?"

"No." Thank God for that.

"Then you have my word. Tell me."

"I have a kid, Austin." The words sounded far too raw when he said them aloud. "An absolutely incredible little baby girl. Her name's Stella."

"You what?"

Nolan hoped no one else was in his brother's vicinity as he yelled the words.

"How old is she?"

"Three months."

"And I'm just now hearing about it? It took you this long to figure out you had to do something about it?" Austin's tone was still loud enough for Nolan to hear every word with his cell phone held out at arm's length.

"I didn't know about her myself until last week," he said, pulling his arm back in so he could talk into the phone. "And please stop yelling. I'm not a kid anymore and don't need you ragging on me. Believe me, I'm doing enough of that myself."

"Jeez, man, a kid?"

"I know. She's phenomenal, Austin. I never knew it was possible to instantly love something like this, but I have to take care of her." He wasn't articulating at all as he'd planned. Just spewing the emotion bottled up inside him.

"Are you sure she's yours?"

The quiet words stopped him in his tracks. Literally. Standing in the middle of the somewhat-dingy hotel room, he looked in the mirror across from the bed. He saw himself, a successful banker, standing there, and hardly recognized the man.

But he felt like him.

"Positive."

"You've had a paternity test, then, good."

"No, I haven't had a paternity test! She's mine."

"You don't know that, bro. Women have been using kids to trap rich men for centuries. Doing the math, I'm guessing you're wherever you were last Christmas, seeing her again."

"Lizzie isn't like that, Austin. I know…you didn't think Kelly was, either, but I swear to you. What this woman wants most is for me to leave her alone."

"That's what she says. And let me guess, you've already offered her support."

"That baby is my responsibility. Of course I'm going to take care of her."

"She's playing you, Nolan."

Austin sounded as sure about that as Nolan was sure she wasn't.

"Remember when I first told the family I was married? No one liked Kelly. But I was absolutely certain you all just had to get to know her. Sure that I knew her. She was my soul mate, Nolan. I was so sure of it I was willing to risk the Fortune name, our money…"

His brother let the words speak for themselves. Nolan knew where the story ended. How it ended.

Only the fact that his wife had been a proven player had saved Austin from losing a whole lot more money than he had.

"You couldn't possibly feel surer than I did then, Nolan. I'd have died for the woman."

Yep, that about summed it up.

"I'm telling you, before you do another thing, and— Wait…you haven't signed anything yet, have you?"

An offer on a house, but he had a ten-day inspection period to get out of that, a period he'd planned to waive. He'd only put down a thousand bucks, in any event. If he didn't follow through on the deal, he'd only be out that much.

Until the house closed, he was covered.

"No."

"Good. That's real good. So now, before you do another thing, you get that paternity test done. You don't even have a problem until that comes back—and I'm betting that when it does, you'll find that you don't have a problem at all."

He did not want to ask Lizzie for a paternity test.

"Hey, at least promise this…" Austin was saying. "Promise me you won't sign anything until after you're home tomorrow. We'll talk then."

Yeah, about that… He didn't even know if he was going to New Orleans.

He had the ticket. Everyone was expecting him to show up.

But he couldn't see a way to leave Lizzie and Stella. It was the baby's first Christmas. And Lizzie…well, he wanted to be there with her.

"I can give you my word I won't sign anything before tomorrow," he said.

His days of "freedom" were quickly drawing to a premature close. He was buying a house. Planning to support a woman and child. He had to tell his family.

They'd want the paternity test. Which meant asking Lizzie about it.

And telling her that he was no longer keeping her and Stella a secret.

How could he hope to do any of that when even the small things were stumping him? Was he going home for Christmas or not?

Either way, he was going to be letting someone down and needed to let them know.

He knew what he wanted to do—spend Christmas with Lizzie. But his decisions didn't just affect himself. Whatever he did reflected on his family, as well. And could put the family's personal fortune at risk—as Austin had done.

Yearnings, wants—those were kid stuff.

It was time for him to man-up.

Chapter Eighteen

Waking up with a feeling of excitement Monday morning, Lizzie took time to wash and blow-dry her hair, leaving it long and wavy. She put on makeup, her favorite pair of leggings and a long, red, figure-hugging sweater with a sequined mantel on the front holding Christmas stockings. Nolan had bought it for her at a boutique they'd happened on the year before—not that he'd necessarily remember that.

Stella's outfit, also from Nolan, was black leggings and a red dress, with a reindeer on the front—and matching bow to clip onto her hairband. Perfect for a visit with Santa.

She wasn't sure what to make of Nolan's pants and tie, the fancy shoes, but Carmela left no doubt of her reaction as she approached him holding the door open for her to climb into the back of the SUV next to Stella's car seat.

"Wow. Impressive, Fortune," she said, not all that

kindly. Lizzie shot her a look, a silent *Please?* And Carmela nodded as she buckled herself in.

She and Carmela had had a long talk the night before when Lizzie had returned from the club. Carmela was certain that Lizzie was in love with Stella's father. She just didn't trust the man. He was setting Lizzie up like a kept woman and Carmela didn't approve. At all. Even when Lizzie tried, over and over, to assure her friend that she wouldn't marry Nolan even if he asked. She wanted no part of his fancy, high-powered life in New Orleans.

The rest—being in love with the man—she'd learn to live with. She just needed time.

And to have her brain about her apparently. "I forgot the diaper bag," she announced from the front seat, just as Nolan was starting the vehicle.

She opened her door, but he insisted that he'd go get it.

Afraid to leave him and Carmela alone in the vehicle together, not counting a sleeping Stella, who would neither distract nor be able to referee, Lizzie handed him her house key.

"I have one question for you," Carmela asked as Lizzie watched Nolan, looking a new kind of hot to her, walking across the parking lot.

"What?"

"If you love him, really love him, don't you have to love the Fortune part, too, not just the Forte?"

She didn't know. But she feared whether she had to or not didn't matter. It was becoming pretty clear to her that she already did. She let her silence speak for itself.

"And that being the case," Carmela continued, "wouldn't that mean at least trying to like New Orleans?"

Her chest tightened and Lizzie's good mood evaporated. "You know me, Carm. You really think I'd be happy there? Living in their atmosphere?"

"No. You hate attention."

She hated pity even more, not that anyone was offering her any. She'd learned a long time ago to keep her private life private. She'd been truly happy for the first time in years when she'd come to college and escaped the persona of the "poor, sweet little girl who'd lost both of her parents so tragically."

The plane crash had been all over the news. The weekend ski trip, the well-to-do Mahoneys and their friends, a couple from Chicago, a friend of Barbara Mahoney's from high school, in a private jet. Her parents hadn't even been named. Just "a couple," "a friend of Barbara's." The news had talked about the Mahoneys' assets, about siblings who'd fought over them. It had never mentioned the little girl who'd been left with nothing but an aunt who'd loved her enough to take her in, but who'd had to struggle financially to do so. There'd been no basis for any kind of lawsuit and it wasn't like her parents had been insured for such a catastrophe. Their life insurance policies had only covered funeral expenses.

"It doesn't matter," she said, putting a halt to her thoughts, something she'd learned to do out of self-preservation many years before. She'd had the world, even after she lost her parents, because she'd had love. "He's not going to ask. Now, can we please just have fun today?"

The path to joy was learning to find it in the little things. In the life she had. In the choices that were her own. The things she could effect.

"Of course," Carmela said. "Do I get to have a picture with Stella and Santa?"

* * *

As it turned out, Stella didn't like Santa. Stiffening the second Lizzie placed her on his lap, she started to cry, and Lizzie ended up holding her while Lizzie sat on Santa's knee. Carmela jumped in on Santa's other side for a shot, but when Santa's helper asked Nolan if he wanted to come up, he shook his head. He was busy taking shots from his cell phone.

Nolan loved being with Lizzie, being a part of Stella's Christmas firsts. He cataloged as much as he could, knowing that, if nothing else, he'd always have the pictures. With Carmela along there was no time for personal conversation with Lizzie and his time had run out. Either he was on the plane the next day or he wasn't.

Which was why, when they pulled into the apartment complex with just enough time for him to get back to his hotel room and change—hopefully without running into his bandmates so he wouldn't have to explain the clothes—he grabbed Lizzie for a quick conversation before he took off.

"Can we…talk tonight? I can come by as soon as I'm done at the club."

Her easy expression instantly stiffening, she asked, "Why? What's wrong?"

"Nothing's wrong," he quickly assured her, praying that she'd still see it that way when she heard what he had to say, that he'd come up with something that would please everyone who was counting on him. "I just… We've got so much going on, we're doing so much, making life-changing decisions, and I'd just like to talk. You know, you and me. To make sure we're both on the same page."

True. All true.

"Okay," she said, nodding, seeming to relax again. And he took that as a good sign.

He was still telling himself the changes in her since they'd reached their agreement and purchased the house—the way she'd let him hold the baby, and then taught him to change her, the way she'd given him her key and let him go back to the apartment for the diaper bag—were all good signs as he walked to her place hours later as soon as the band wrapped up.

Because they weren't playing Christmas Eve or Christmas Day, he was carrying his horn with him. Daly and Glenn were staying at the hotel over the holiday. Branham was on a late-night flight back to his hometown of Baton Rouge.

Nolan had texted Lizzie, just like she'd asked, when he was out front, and, in jeans and a zipped-up dark hoodie, she came out to join him. As if by telepathic communication, they started walking down the block together, toward a small park that had a lighted fountain in the middle of it. It was a walk they'd taken before, several times, before going back to her place after a night at the club.

It never had been just all about sex for them.

Though, man, the sex had been incredible...

"Thank you for coming out so late," he started in, still not certain where the conversation was going to end up. Only that he'd determined he couldn't make the Christmas decision until he talked to her.

He felt her shrug next to his shoulder, hadn't realized they were walking that close, but he reached down and took her hand.

When she didn't pull immediately away, he walked in silence for a few seconds. There was a nip in the air, but it was more cool than cold.

"How was the club tonight?" she asked, and he took hope from the fact that she wasn't asking him to get to his point.

"Crowded. I think the band's going to be asked back next year."

Campus was pretty deserted, but the area surrounding it, even this late, had enough holiday revelers about that he felt completely comfortable. The cop car parked close by, and the security officers patrolling, helped, too.

They'd reached a bench by the fountain. She let go of his hand as they sat and he had to say, "I've missed you so much, Lizzie. I wish you could know how much. I know it doesn't seem like it, I know my actions look differently, but I've spent this entire year trying to get out from under your spell."

The streetlights and the lights from the fountain weren't brilliant, but they illuminated her eyes as he gazed straight into them. Another couple walked close by, milling around the other side of the fountain, and still he felt like he and Lizzie were shut off from the world.

He wished they were.

Raising a hand to his face, she touched his cheek. "You confuse me," she said softly.

"You are so beautiful," he told her. If this was his moment, if his truth was going to be heard, it had to start with that which was deepest inside himself.

Leaning in slowly, he touched his lips to hers. Not with forethought. Or any thought, really. It just happened. She allowed the kiss and, seconds later, opened her lips to allow him to reacquaint himself with her more intimately. It was a hello.

Not a goodbye.

The thought infiltrated and Nolan pulled back.

"I'm sorry," he said, needing to lean his head against hers for a second, but not doing so. He didn't touch her. "I respect your need for no physical relationship between us." He wanted to promise it would never happen again, but couldn't make any more promises he wasn't sure he could keep.

"It's…okay," she said, sounding like the Lizzie he'd known the year before. Her voice was filled with… something… He didn't know what. But it sank into him and nestled down. "I mean, I still meant what I said, but…it was one kiss and we stopped. We were lovers, Nolan. And, as far as I was concerned, it was pretty incredible. We can't dance around that fact if we're going to make this work."

Pretty incredible. At her words, desire shot through him.

"Making love with you was like nothing I've ever known," he said. "It was so much more than sex. I think that's why it's been so hard for me to get you out of my system."

Whoa with the honesty there, buddy. He couldn't afford for this to go backward on him.

"I don't know what to say." She was still looking at him.

"It's the truth."

He couldn't tell if it was the lights, or if a sudden sheen of tears had come to her eyes. He knew only that her expression changed.

"And now we have to put Stella first," she said. "We have to handle whatever past business there is between us, put the past behind us, so that we can provide for her. We're two responsible parents, not lovers sharing a two-week idyll. If we had sex again, so many other feelings would be involved, like I'd start to get jealous when you go home to New Orleans, worry about what women might be there… It would get awful and then where would that leave Stella?"

And there they were, right at the point he'd been dreading. He still couldn't find a way to ask her for a paternity test.

Maybe they had to build up to that point.

When she shivered, he asked, "You want to go back?"

Nodding, she stood. "Do you mind? It's colder than I thought. You could come in, have some tea. Carmela knows you might. She won't bother us."

At that point, he almost wished her roommate would join them. He'd have to focus on the facts before him, not the woman he so desperately needed.

He didn't take her hand as they walked back to her place, but he stayed close enough that their arms touched, and their hips bumped a time or two.

He needed this…to be connected to her…sex or not. She was the mother of his child. And so much more.

Carmela had been right. If Lizzie really loved Nolan, she had to consider him in their mix, too. The realization helped her as they climbed the stairs to her apartment and she let him inside. Fighting her feelings for him, fearing them, weren't going to make them go away. She had to face them head-on. Deal with them. So that they could find a way to coexist without burning each other to bits.

Parents who hated each other weren't going to be good for Stella.

Allowing herself to admit she loved him…what a relief. And now she had to find a way to live with her sexual attraction to him without letting it get in the way and ruin them.

A tall order.

She poured tea while she pondered it.

She handed him a cup and followed him into the living room. They were talking in whispers, and she took a detour to close Carmela's door. Her friend, if she awoke, would understand.

She checked on Stella, too. Because she couldn't resist. The baby girl, in a new red fleece sleeper, was on her back, sound asleep, mouth open.

So precious. Innocent. Completely dependent.

"I love you, baby girl," she whispered, and turned to head back in to Nolan, only to find him in the bedroom doorway, looking in on them. Stepping aside, she motioned him over, and they stood there together, watching their daughter sleep, until he finally took her hand to lead her back down the hall.

They sat on the couch together. Lizzie would have chosen the chair, but this was new ground—space where they were admitting they had feelings for each other, while they worked through a way to deal with them without acting on them. It was a recipe for disaster, given the obvious chemistry that still flared between them. She wanted to get married someday. And she assumed he did, too. There was no way it could work between them, though. She could never fit into his world, and she had to make him realize that. Eventually they'd end up hurting each other. Hating each other.

How could anything like this possibly work out?

Anyway, she didn't know the answer, but felt certain that, together, they could find it. Because of Stella.

As he had earlier, he took her hand. She didn't pull

back. Carmela was just down the hall. More to the point, so was Stella.

Could they love each other, openly, without sex?

She desperately wanted for there to be a way.

"I think it's pretty clear that what we had last year still lives between us," he started. Her lips were trembling as she smiled and nodded.

"I hope knowing that will help you understand the struggle within me." His eyes were so serious, so filled with warmth...and pain? She couldn't tear her gaze away.

"I can't not be Nolan Fortune," he told her. And her heart melted for him. All over him.

"Nolan, is that what this about?" she asked him. "I'm not going to ask you, or expect you, or even hope that you would ever turn your back on who you are. I knew from the second you told me who you were that Nolan Fortune is who you have to be." Suddenly Carmela's words meant so much more than she'd understood at the time. "I care for you, Nolan. I couldn't possibly do that and ask you to be someone you aren't."

He didn't look as appeased, or relieved, as she'd hoped he would.

"I mean it. I know you have to go back. That your life is there. Your family is there. I won't ever stand in the way of that."

"I have to tell them about Stella."

Her stomach clenched, but she hung in there. How good was their future if she was felled at the first challenge?

"I know," she said. She'd always known. "But you'll stick to our agreement, right?"

"About the house?"

Her breathing was coming in short spurts now, but she was going to persevere.

"And about her living with me and you visiting?"

She had to make certain that her part of that negotiation remained solid. It was all that could really matter to her.

"Yes," he said. "Absolutely." With those two words, everything inside Lizzie settled into place. He really was going to honor her need to mother their daughter full-time.

"So, I'm officially out from under my promise to keep her a secret," he said, as though full disclosure was the only thing he was worried about. For herself, she'd been frantic that his family would take Stella away from her.

Reeling herself in, Lizzie nodded. Nolan was a strong man. He was a man his family could rely on, but that made him a man she could rely on, too. He knew their situation. He wasn't going to let his family convince him otherwise.

Or was she trying to squash her concerns now, just to get along? Life was just so hard sometimes. It shouldn't be so complicated.

She made herself admit the truth. "I'm scared, Nolan. I'm afraid that you'll tell them and they'll want Stella and convince you to fight me for custody. With your money, I won't have a hope in hell of fighting back."

He sat back, shook his head. "What have I ever done to make you think I'd take her away from you?" he asked, sounding hurt. "I know you have a thing about money and the supposed power it brings, along with the chains it imposes, but come on, Lizzie. You and Stella mean so much to me. You *and* Stella. She needs you. And even if she didn't, I wouldn't hurt you that way.

I've never even had a thought about taking her from you. You're a great mother, Lizzie. As her daddy, how could I want anyone but you caring for her?"

She'd never thought of it that way. Not ever. Tears filled her eyes, but she didn't look away from him. He had to get through the tough moments. Not avoid them.

He wiped at the tears that had fallen on her cheeks. "I think we just crossed our first hurdle," he told her. "I fully intend, with every fiber of my being, to make sure that both you and Stella are happy."

She smiled at him. Reached up to take ahold of the arm he'd lifted to her face. "Thank you. I will do everything I can to help you be happy, too," she said. Then she leaned toward him.

And he kissed her.

He wasn't leaving in the morning. He wasn't going home for Christmas. He wasn't asking for a paternity test. Funny how the answers had all come to him.

With his lips all over Lizzie's, his tongue mating hungrily with hers, Nolan knew he was right where he needed to be. He kissed the corners of her mouth, and then she whimpered and moved her face, greedily seeking his lips again. Her body was pressing into him and he pulled her with him until they were lying down on the couch with her on top of him.

God, it felt good. So damned incredibly good. His hard-on pressed into her and she pressed right back. It had been a year too long since he'd felt so…right. Reaching between them, she touched the swollen bulge beneath his fly and he almost came apart.

He lifted a hand to her breast and…stopped. It was hard, not at all the pliable flesh he knew. Because it was filled with milk.

A reality check.

He wanted to believe he pulled away first, but knew it was her. He'd stopped moving his hand on her, but he'd still been kissing her like crazy. Pushing against him, she moaned as she sat up and landed in the chair next to the couch.

"Oh, my God," she said, her head in her hands. She was shaking.

So was he.

"I'm sorry." He didn't know what else to say.

"It's not your fault..." Her voice faltered. "I just... We have to make this work, Nolan. I want it to work. I just... I think...maybe we've been spending too much time together all at once. Too much like last year. Taking things too fast."

He knew she was right.

Felt it, too.

His mind and his heart were finally in sync.

"I think I'm going to go home for Christmas," he told her. He knew he was. "I'm going to tell my parents about you and Stella and about our plans. The fact that I'm not abandoning them for Christmas will help them be more amenable. I'll be back on the twenty-sixth. I have to play later that night, but I'll come and see you and Stella the second I get back."

There were no tears in her eyes as she looked up at him, but her gaze was stricken with so much more emotion than he was equipped to handle at that moment.

She nodded.

"I mean it, Lizzie, I'll be back this time."

Another halfhearted nod was her only response.

Swearing, he pulled out his wallet, grabbed the first nonplastic card he found—his country club membership—found a pen and wrote down his home address, both of his parents' cell numbers and his own office number, before dropping the card on the coffee table.

He wanted to haul her up into his arms. To hold on tight and promise her that everything would be all right.

But he didn't trust himself to let her go again. So he did the only thing left.

He let himself out.

Chapter Nineteen

The next morning, Carmela took one look at Lizzie's face as she wandered into the kitchen after putting a recently fed Stella in her swing, and demanded to know what had happened. Then she took charge.

"He is not going to take Stella away from you," she said when Lizzie told her what she most feared. "You definitely have reason to mistrust him, sweetie, but his money and supposed power aside, has he ever even indicated that he'd want to have Stella half the time?"

Still in her sleep pants and T-shirt, Lizzie shook her head. Listening. Desperate for reason that made sense to shut out the panic-ridden thoughts in her brain.

She knew she was overreacting. She just couldn't seem to stop. It wasn't like her. At all.

"I'd think a more likely fear," Carmela said, "would be that his parents are going to convince him you're a gold digger and try to get him to have nothing more to do with either you or Stella."

That was a viable possibility, for sure. And if that did happen, she'd be home free.

But her heart sank and tears sprang to her eyes.

"That's what's really happening, isn't it?" she asked. "He's ditching me again."

It shouldn't hurt so much. She had Stella. She didn't need him.

Oh, God, why did it hurt so much to think that she wasn't good enough for a man who'd run out on her once already?

What was wrong with her that she'd still love him?

"I don't know." Carmela's words reached her through a haze of pain.

She looked up from her seat, slumped at the table, as her friend scrambled eggs for them, meeting Carmela's gaze. Carmela hated Nolan. Or close to it. She didn't trust him. She was the one who'd known from the beginning that he was just using Lizzie. That he wouldn't ever call again after he left the previous year.

She'd been right all along.

"It's odd that he left this, don't you think?" Carmela asked, holding up the card that Lizzie had left right where Nolan had dropped it the night before, on the coffee table. Her friend had obviously picked it up that morning since it was now in the kitchen.

She stared at the card, trying not to remember how good it had felt to have Nolan's body moving under hers just moments before he jotted those phone numbers.

"He gave you his mom and dad's cell phone numbers," Carmela said. "It doesn't get any more real than that."

"He gave me numbers, Carm," she said. "Just like last time. Who knows if they're really to his parents' cells? Or if he'll warn them to disconnect them?" She'd uttered those questions for hours as she'd lain awake in the dark of the night, trying to figure out exactly what was going on, and where she was making mistakes.

"And it's not like I'm going to call them to check," she added, though she'd thought about doing so.

"He left his office number. You could call that. See where it gets you." She could. And might, sometime, if she really needed to reach him.

It would have to be a pretty severe emergency, though. She'd promised herself that.

"And his pass to get into his country club," Carmela added, reading the other side of the card. Lizzie hadn't picked the thing up, hadn't known what it was.

Of course he'd have membership to a country club. And he probably didn't physically need the pass. They'd know who he was.

A country club...

While her parents hadn't qualified as members, they'd been frequent guests at the Mahoneys' country club in Chicago. She remembered how her mom would rave afterward about the food they ate, and then complain about the boxed hamburger meals that Lizzie had grown to love.

"Did he say when he'd be back?" Carmela's question broke into her thoughts. Details of her life as a child didn't define her anymore.

"Thursday sometime," Lizzie told her. "Said he'd stop here before going to the club, but wasn't sure how much time he'd have."

"The day after Christmas," Carmela said as though that had some significance. "He's planning to come right back, Lizzie. What if he really was just going home to break the news of you and Stella to his family? I can't imagine it's going to be easy for him. Not only laying his new family on them, but also telling them that you all aren't going to be a family...in the traditional sense."

And if they demanded that he end his association with her and Stella? Would he? Would he walk away from them and deny Stella the right to know her father?

It was a better proposition than having them come after her for partial custody, right?

After all, Lizzie would be getting what she wanted. The assurance that Stella would grow up full-time with her. That's all that mattered.

She'd told herself so many times.

So why, with her daughter sleeping in the very next room, was she struggling so hard to find her joy?

Nolan could have called for a car to be waiting for him at the airport. He'd flown first-class, as usual. He could have messaged from the plane.

He took a cab instead. He was going to do this on his terms. From his arrival to his departure, he was the one in charge. So he was the youngest of four boys, he was a grown man.

And the first of them to become a father.

Thinking of that little baby girl, at home in her Pack 'n Play, in her car seat, on her changing table, in his arms, he knew it was time for him to adjust his thinking about his place in the family once and for all. He didn't have to work harder than the rest. Didn't have to prove a damned thing to them.

He'd always carried his weight, and then some, and would continue to do so.

He was also going to provide for Lizzie and Stella. Period.

With that thought firmly in mind he skipped the stop-off at his own luxury condominium and instructed the cabbie to take him straight to the mansion he'd grown up in. He walked in the front door unannounced, letting himself in with his own key.

He'd told his mother not to expect him until after the family dinner that preceded the small party with close friends every year—a sit-down meal at one table that included only Miles and Sarah, his parents, and their seven children. He'd lingered at the airport bar after his plane had landed so that he timed his arrival accordingly.

Or would have, had he not suddenly opted to skip the condo part of his plan. He'd thought he'd drop off his suitcase, shower and change. The horn had to go with him.

Showing up for Christmas Eve in pants and shirt wrinkled from travel wasn't all that respectful, but he was there in New Orleans when he wanted to be in Austin with Lizzie and Stella, so that was enough.

And dinner with them all together suddenly seemed like the time to make his appearance. Better than the private sit-down with his father he'd been envisioning all along.

His father had just finished saying grace when Nolan made his appearance at the French doors leading into the dining room. His parents and six siblings, all dressed appropriately—the women in expensive red or black dresses that looked the same to him every year even though he knew they'd die before they wore the same dress to a party two years in a row, and the men in dress pants, shirts and ties in some shade of red or green. His mother had a diamond Christmas tree pinned to her red dress. And his father's tie—red with little Christmas trees all over it—was one Belle, the youngest Fortune, had picked out for him when she was little. He'd worn it every year since.

The table, resplendent not only with the traditional ham, potato soufflé, various veggie dishes and bread baskets, was adorned in holiday decor, too, right down to the dishes and silver.

He'd never thought twice about eating on china that was only used two days a year. Paper plates with Lizzie would have suited him.

"Nolan!" His mother, Sarah, jumped up, her napkin falling to her chair as she ran over to give him a hug and a kiss on the cheek. "You made it in time for dinner! And you brought your saxophone! I'm so glad. Come on, have a seat," she said, indicating his normal place at the table. It had been fully set.

Because he'd become that predictable? Was he that much of a "good son"?

Or maybe it was just out of respect for his place at that table.

The second he moved to his chair everyone started talking at once. His sisters at him. His father to his mother. Sarah to Diana, the woman who'd be serving at the party later that evening, as well. She took his bags and returned with a glass of wine, for which he thanked her, giving her a smile and a "Merry Christmas."

It wasn't until she was out of the room that everything changed. Silence fell and all of the food still lay untouched on the table.

Savannah, next to him, nudged him in the thigh under the table with her hand. Younger than him by a year, closest to him in age, she'd been his table mate his entire life. And she was letting him know he was the subject of the silence.

His father cleared his throat and Nolan's grew tight.

He glared to his father's left—Sarah was always on his right rather than at the end of the table—to his oldest brother.

Austin met his gaze with a shrug.

"I presume Austin broke his word to me and told you my news," he said, meeting his father's eyes straight-on.

"Hell, yes, he told me!" Miles's booming voice boomed louder. Banging his hand on the table, he didn't seem to notice the silver and china rattle as he continued. "How could you be so careless, son? I just don't get it."

Georgia, next to Austin, was adjusting her silverware. Belle dropped her napkin and bent to pick it up. Savannah was practically bruising his leg.

Avoiding the disappointment he knew he'd see in his mother's eyes, Nolan addressed the man he'd looked up to and adored his entire life. That moment included.

"Wait just a minute," Sarah said, her hand on Miles's arm when he took a breath, obviously preparing to fire at Nolan again. She looked down the table at him, her eyes wide. "Am I to understand that you fathered a child?" Her voice rose higher with each word.

Five of his six siblings stared at him. Nothing like putting a guy on the spot. On second thought, he realized, he probably should have opted for his first plan—the after-dinner talk alone with his father.

Except…they were a family. His family.

"Yes, Mom, I did," he said, reaching for his phone. There was no way anyone could resist pictures of that sweet little girl in her Christmas garb sitting on Santa's lap.

"You don't know that," Austin butted in. "You have no proof the child is yours."

That made him angry. Bone-deep, punch-his-brother-in-the-face pissed. The other five Fortune heirs had swung their gazes back to him, all wisely silent.

"I know she's mine," he said, letting the phone go. Ignoring his siblings for the moment, he looked between his mother and his father. "To be honest with you, even if Stella wasn't mine—and I know for certain she is— I'd still love her every bit as much. Just as I am help-lessly in love with Lizzie, her mother."

Oh, God, that felt so good. Weights flew off his chest, up to the ether, where he hoped they'd get lost from him forever. Never did he want to live as he had for the past year, carrying around so much...wrong.

No one said a word. Miraculously no one even seemed to move.

"I have a grandchild?" Sarah suddenly blurted. "I'm a grandma?"

With a glance in her direction, Miles turned his at-tention to Nolan. "Are you telling me that you want to keep this woman and child in your life?" he asked.

"Yes," Nolan said. "As a matter of fact, I've already promised her that I will do so."

"You're bringing them here to New Orleans?" Sarah asked. And then she looked toward the door. "Are they here now?"

He knew that if his mother gave Lizzie a chance, she'd love her. If she ever got that chance.

"You've asked her to marry you?" Miles was more to the point.

Nolan shook his head. "She doesn't want to be with me," he told everyone. "She's not wealthy and doesn't want to be. I'm buying a house in Austin and will be flying back and forth to see them whenever I can."

"You can't do that," Sarah said. His brothers Draper

and Beau agreed. In fact, they were all talking to him at the same time.

"Hold on!" Miles quieted everyone. Instantly.

His father looked at him and said, "You are a Fortune, son. I didn't raise you to be a quitter, did I?"

"Excuse me?" He shook his head as he leaned forward, meeting the man eye to eye. "I can't force a woman to marry me," he said. "Nor would I even want to. She wouldn't be happy. I wouldn't be happy. And that would guarantee that Stella wouldn't be happy."

"Stella. How old is she?" Sarah asked.

Grabbing his phone, Nolan scrolled to one of the two photos Lizzie had taken of him holding his daughter for the first time and passed it down to his mother. He'd have liked to stand over her shoulder and gush with her, or watch her reaction even, but he had his father to deal with.

"This isn't one of your business deals, Dad. We're talking about a woman here. And an innocent child. Lizzie's life changed when her parents befriended a wealthy couple. Their priorities changed and she was left alone a lot. She's really intent on living a modest lifestyle, and believes happiness comes from being able to do what you need to do, not what you're expected to do. Beyond that, I screwed up. When I left her last year, I didn't tell her who I really was. I was thinking about Molly and how wrong that went and... I just wanted it to end as a great memory. Instead, I left her to give birth to my child all alone."

"All the more reason for you to fight like hell for what's yours," Miles said, intimidating in spite of the decorated Christmas tie. "We're talking about family here, Nolan, and I will not have history repeat itself. I can't allow it. Not in my home. Not in my family."

It was Nolan's turn to stare, openmouthed. What on earth...?

Miles seemed to change right before his eyes. To deflate. And then, with a long look at Sarah, who nodded, he straightened his shoulders.

"Perhaps it's time," he said.

Savannah laid a hand on Nolan's knee under the table.

"As you know, I grew up in a modest neighborhood here in New Orleans. Your Grandma Melton was a single mother at a time when that was still looked down upon in society. I had an affinity for numbers, and got a scholarship to college, but not the best college. And I wasn't ever invited to join the best fraternities. I learned early that it wasn't just what you knew, but who you knew."

Grandma Melton, much loved by all of them, and still a force in her eighties, would be at the party later, and spend the night to be there with them for Christmas morning, too. As would his mother's parents.

Yeah, they knew all of this. And that his dad had changed his name to Fortune so he'd sound more important and spent the first few years after college working his butt off at a financial services company and learning to blend in with his more affluent colleagues. It was through them that he'd met Sarah Barrington.

"As you also know, when your grandparents asked about my family, I told them I was distantly related to the Fortunes of Texas."

But he'd told Sarah the truth, about his mother, about his name change, and his parents had told them all, individually, when they'd been called in to their father's den for "the talk." In the Fortune family that talk didn't have to do with sex. It was the talk that let them know who and what they were, as a family, and as a member in the family. They'd heard the story. Alone, with just their parents, so they could be free to ask any questions, or express any feelings whatever they might be.

They'd heard about how his father had made his first million by the time Austin was born, and how hard work and honest business dealings had built the Fortune empire they now all carried.

Nolan had been ten when he'd had "the talk." Austin had been eight.

"My father never fought for me," Miles said slowly. "When he found out Grandma Melton was pregnant he suggested that she terminate the pregnancy. Obviously she didn't. She couldn't even think about doing that. After I was born, he said he'd never acknowledge me as his son. And he told her she'd never get a dime out of him for support. Which she did not."

"I…"

"What the…?"

"I can't…"

"That's horrible." Nolan made out Savannah's whole sentence. She was sitting right next to him.

"I'm sorry." Nolan waited until the room grew silent to speak. "I had no idea."

The rest of his siblings sat quietly now, pretty much dumbfounded, Nolan figured. Just like he was.

He gave Savannah's hand a squeeze.

"There's more," Miles said, and Nolan's gaze swung immediately back to him.

"Your mother is the only one who knows this, other than Grandma Melton, but…it's time," he said, repeating the words that had started the bizarre turn this conversation had taken.

Miles looked at Sarah, who, holding his hand now, nodded again.

"I didn't know the identity of my biological father until I graduated from college," he said.

Nolan's jaw dropped. His dad knew who his dad was?

Part of the whole talk was about him not knowing… about the hard times they'd had with Grandma Melton being a single mom in times when that was frowned upon and…

He glanced around the table, needing his siblings for a second. They were all watching Miles.

"It was probably clear to her at that point that I felt like I was going to have to work harder for less, that I was facing a life with fewer chances, because of being a nobody. She wanted me to be proud of the man I was." He shook his head, looking older than Nolan had ever noticed. "I was a kid, didn't get yet that the man you are is defined by your choices, about what you do, not about who sired you."

"Who's your father, Dad?" Austin asked.

Miles looked first at him, and then around the table at all of them. "I changed my name to Fortune because my father is a Fortune," he said, pausing when every one of them gasped.

What? Nolan wanted to blurt the word. He didn't. He respected his father too much to give him an outburst when the man was clearly struggling and needed support.

"His name was Julius Fortune. He was a wealthy stockbroker who lived in New York."

"Wait a minute…" Austin said, eyes wide. "The father of Jerome Fortune, from the Fortunes of Texas? He's your father?"

Everyone stared. Except Sarah. She nodded.

Nolan was having a hard time taking it in. Questions shot off in his head, one after the other.

"We're really related to *those* Fortunes?" Belle asked, echoing one of his queries. "So…like…what—the Fortunes of Texas are our cousins or something?"

"Yes, but they don't know that," Miles said in a rush. "Grandmother and Grandfather Barrington don't even know. We're nothing like those other Fortunes…"

Nolan's mind spun. The Fortunes had been in the news two years before as a reporter followed them around. Jerome Fortune, another one of Julius's sons, had been living under an assumed name—as Gerald Robinson; he'd built a tech empire in Austin, Texas. And, like his father, he had fathered a lot of children—both legitimate and illegitimate. They'd been finding each other over the past couple of years.

And one of them—an architect from England—upon finding out he was a Fortune, had moved to Texas to help his newfound brother find the rest of their siblings. That architect was Keaton Whitfield…

"Lizzie has a roommate who is a fifth year architect student interning with one of Jerome's illegitimate sons—Keaton Fortune Whitfield."

Every head swung his way. It struck him then that their guests would be arriving soon to find the host family sitting at the table with their mouths open staring at each other. Nolan couldn't shake the mental picture.

He'd like to find a way to edit himself out of it. But he was in too deep. Permanently in. This was his family.

And he'd just brought the attention back to the fact that he, like his grandfather before him apparently, had sired an illegitimate child.

"Nolan, you get yourself back to Austin and let that

family you've started know that they are a loved and accepted part of this family. Find a way to get them home to us."

His father was demanding the impossible. This wasn't the dark ages where he could go grab Lizzie and haul her off to his cave. But he'd just been granted the one thing he'd wished for for Christmas—a ticket back to Austin to be a part of Stella's first Christmas. With his family's blessing.

"Can I take the private plane?" he asked his father.

"Just make sure you have her on it with you when you come home," Miles said.

"And please don't say anything about your father, about the Fortunes, until we've had a chance to let your grandparents know," Sarah said, which was the official "this talk is over" signal.

His six siblings started talking at once. All with questions directed at Nolan.

But he stood up. He had a flight to arrange.

Chapter Twenty

Lizzie had a text from Nolan on Christmas Eve telling her that he'd arrived safely. She wished him a happy holiday.

With Christmas music on, she and Carmela wrapped presents most of the evening, even wrapping up the things Nolan had bought for the baby that she hadn't yet worn or used, so there'd be loads of packages under the tree for pictures. She wanted her little girl to know, when she looked at the photos of her first Christmas, that she was greatly loved and showered with gifts.

She only had a couple of pictures of her own first Christmas but the tree had been overflowing, in spite of her parents' modest lifestyle, and she'd known her entire life how much they'd celebrated her, loved her, wanted her. Those little gifts, sometimes just the socks and underwear she needed, had meant more to her than any of the fancy, expensive toys the Mahoneys had bought for her.

Carmela got a call sometime after ten, and when Lizzie got up to turn down the music so she could hear, she shook her head and went back to her room. Stella, who'd fallen asleep in her swing, woke up soon after and Lizzie sat in front of the lighted tree, bows and tinsel glistening, as she fed her daughter.

She missed Nolan. Horribly. And yet…she was so lucky, she reminded herself. Had so much more than so many. She could do this. She could be a single mom. Raise Stella with or without Nolan coming for visits. In his house, in a home he'd provide. She just hadn't figured out how to stop loving a man who was so unsuited to her.

Hadn't figured out how to have him around and not fall further in love. Or need him more.

Wiping away the stupid tears that had been slipping out on and off throughout the day, she burped Stella, changed her and put her down in her Pack 'n Play.

"Go to sleep, little one, and Santa will come to bless you with miracles," she whispered, words that came to her from the distant past. She'd forgotten that her mom used to say those words to her on Christmas Eve.

So much of the years with her parents were pushed deeply inside her, not allowed out, for fear that they'd crush her with sorrow. As a kid, pushing away the memories was the only way she'd been able to cope with the loss of her family and somehow the practice had become habit until she didn't even know she was doing it anymore.

But having Stella, being a mom, was bringing it all out. Maybe more quickly than she was ready for.

Back out in the living area, she made her and Carmela cups of tea, and then, in red flannel pants and a black long-sleeved T-shirt, she sat barefoot on the couch with all of the lights off but for the Christmas tree that put out a colorful glow. She'd turned the music down some, but left on the Christmas tunes and waited for her friend to join her.

"Is Stella down for the night?" Carmela asked, coming out in her pj's a few minutes later.

"Yeah." For several hours at least. She hoped. The baby had been doing much better the past week, giving Lizzie six-hour stretches during the night.

"So what time are we getting up to do this shindig?" Carmela, still standing in the middle of the room, waved toward the tree.

"Early," Lizzie said, grinning. "My parents used to wake me up at the crack of dawn and pretend that it was me who couldn't wait to open presents."

"You kidding?" Carmela grinned. "I was up in the middle of the night trying to get mine up!"

"I made you some tea."

"Yeah... I, um, think I'm going to head on into bed," she said, picking up the tea. "But thanks. Wake me for presents!" Carrying the tea down the hall with her, she was gone. Before eleven.

And Lizzie was alone.

So alone.

The year before had been the first she hadn't made it back to Chicago, to Aunt Betty's, for Christmas. But Nolan had been there with her and she'd figured it for just about the best Christmas ever.

And next year, Stella would be walking, playing with toys. She might still not be aware enough to know who Santa was, but she'd be engaged. Lizzie just had to get through this one year and—

She jumped at the sound of knocking at the door. She

glanced toward it, then down the hall. Carmela wouldn't have gone to bed if she was expecting anyone.

The knock came a second time and she got up, moved toward the door, looked through the peephole and then started to cry again.

It couldn't be.

What was he doing there?

Wiping her eyes, she pulled open the door and Nolan stood there, in wrinkled clothes, the knot of his tie loosened down to his chest, a duffel over his shoulder, a big bag of what looked like wrapped packages as well as his sax case in one hand and an envelope in the other.

"What are you doing here?"

"First off, delivering this," he said, handing her the envelope. He didn't come in. Just stood there on the doorstep, holding his gear.

"You want to come in?"

"Open it." His brown eyes were serious as he nodded toward the envelope and then looked back at her.

The business-size envelope held one piece of paper.

I, Nolan Fortune, tender my parental rights of my child, Stella Sullivan, to her mother, Elizabeth Sullivan.

His signature followed.

Her heart sank.

"I don't understand." Was he just giving up? Walking away from them?

Again?

"May I come in now? Carmela knows I was on my way."

She had no reason to deny him. Except that her heart was breaking.

Sitting on the couch, Lizzie watched as he dropped his satchel and sax by the door and then brought the bag of gifts over. He sat, too. Not too close, but not far away, either.

Her heart was beating so hard she could feel the rhythm in her chest. She swallowed some tea and almost choked.

"Are you going home?" she asked him. He'd said he'd be back the day after Christmas. Did that mean he hadn't left yet? That he'd been shopping for Stella and was on his way to the airport? But he'd texted earlier...

"I've already been."

And he was back so soon? Everything about the night was confusing her. The way she felt. What she wanted. What he wanted.

He pulled a smallish box off the top of the pile in the bag and handed it to her. "This is from my sister Belle. She's the youngest. She's twenty-three."

She didn't take the box. "Don't you want to put that under the tree? Stella's gifts are all under there."

"It's for you." He laid it on her lap.

She stared at him, his face shadowed in the soft glow from the Christmas tree. She'd have turned on more lights, but didn't want him seeing her so well in case she started to cry again.

"Your family knows about me?"

"That was my reason for going back. To tell them all about you and Stella. To let them know that while I am and will always be a Fortune, you and Stella come first."

Had he lost his mind? Or was she losing hers?

"Open it," he said, leaning forward with his forearms resting on his knees as he waited.

Mostly because she had no idea what to do, had nothing coherent to say, Lizzie opened the pretty red-and-gold holiday paper to reveal a white generic gift box.

Pulling the lid off slowly, afraid to look inside, she saw only a photo inside. An old one. Taken from a camera and developed rather than printed. It was of a little boy—four, maybe—dressed in gray pants, a white shirt, a gray jacket, red tie and shiny black shoes. He was holding a little plastic Flutophone.

"He's absolutely adorable," she said. "But who is he?"

She glanced over at Nolan.

"That's me. I'd just won my first talent show playing 'Jingle Bells' on a toy my brother Beau got for Christmas. I was three."

Emotion welled in her again. All day long it had been happening. She'd think she was pregnant, except she'd slept with no one since Nolan last year. "I love it," she said, though she had no idea why Nolan's little sister would want her to have it. "Tell her thank you."

He handed her a second box. "That's from Savannah. She's a year younger than I am and probably the sibling I'm closest to. She's small, but as strong and determined as they come."

Slowly opening the paper—white with Santas all over it, this time—trying to untape rather than rip, she found another generic white box, this one flat and a little bigger.

Inside was a small model plane with a broken wing. The painted detail on the thing was impressive, but...a broken toy? She glanced up at him.

"I made that when I was ten. Took me over a week after school and on weekends. Savannah broke it ten minutes after I finished. I'd forgotten all about it, but she kept it all these years. Says it's a reminder to her that it's better to control your anger than unleash it and lash out. Which was what she'd been doing when she broke it." He coughed. "She, uh, told me to tell you that the reason she learned that was because while I, um, cried when it happened, I just calmly picked up the pieces and walked away. She'd been wanting a fight and I didn't give it to her."

"Why was she so mad at you?"

"I'd read her diary and told one of our brothers that she had a crush on one of his friends."

Oh, my. Hands trembling, she put the plane carefully back in the box. "Please tell her I said thank you." She decided to give the plane back to her. Lizzie wasn't taking anyone's prized possessions.

"This one's from Georgia. She's older than me by two years. And beautiful, but kind of bossy if you ask me."

Inside that box was a drawing he'd made when he was three. The only thing legible was an X and what looked like an O. She'd told him that was how you spelled *I love you*, Nolan explained.

There were boxes from his brothers, too. Beau, who was thirty, Draper, thirty-one, and Austin, who Lizzie had already heard about and was the oldest at thirty-three. One held a can of peas, along with the message that Nolan hated peas so much he'd once left the dinner table and spit them out in his dresser drawer, where they stayed until long after they'd dried up. Another was a rolled-up scroll that turned out to be the first song Nolan had ever written. And the last, which maybe was the oddest of all. *A pair of old cotton pants*. It was from Austin.

"What's this?" she asked.

"The pants I wear around the house the most at

home. Mom has nagged me to get rid of them, but I don't. They're comfortable and I like them."

Overwhelmed, she looked at the open boxes on the couch and table around her. It was so sweet, but what was she supposed to do with all of this stuff?

"You don't get it, do you?" Nolan asked, taking her hand.

Looking at him, starting to cry again, she shook her head.

"I had you open the envelope first because I want you to know—always, first and foremost—that I will never, ever try to keep you out of Stella's life. She's your daughter. You're her mother. That's sacred."

Her chin was trembling now. She couldn't talk.

So she listened as he told her what he'd found out that night about his father. His family. Carmela's boss was his cousin? That went right over her head. Nolan was a famous Fortune? It was too much. Way too much.

"So now you see, no one in my family would ever, ever take Stella from her mother. They just don't want her to be separated from her father, either."

She didn't want that, either, but...

"And now you know that you don't have to agree to anything else in order to keep her," he added.

She was reeling from his revelation, and could only imagine how shocked he was. His entire family was. And yet, his siblings had made presents for her...

"The gifts..."

"My siblings are trying to show you—all except the peas, maybe—that I'm a good guy. I was talking to my dad, making arrangements to get back here, and I didn't know what they were doing until they were done, but they made me swear that I'd give them to you first. Insurance, maybe. Or they were afraid I'd blow it."

"Blow what?"

"I want you to marry me, Lizzie. To come to New Orleans with me, find the house you want to live in there and be my family. You and Stella."

Oh, God.

Oh, God.

She couldn't breathe. She'd told Carmela multiple times that if he asked, she'd say no.

"At least come back for Christmas dinner. Mom and Dad are going to call you and ask if I can't get you to say yes."

"That's tomorrow!" she said. "We can't possibly get a flight in so little time and—"

She couldn't quit shaking.

"The plane's ready and waiting whenever we are," he was saying. "Carmela said you were opening gifts in the morning and then she was going to catch a flight out to see her family. I was thinking we could leave when she does. It's only an hour-and-a-half flight..."

She was hearing more white noise than him. "What plane?"

"The family plane," he told her. "Russell, our pilot, will head back home tonight and be here tomorrow at whatever time we need. His ex has their kids over Christmas this year and he was at a loose end..."

That was it. The end.

"I...can't," Lizzie said, standing, and then when she was hit with a swoosh of light-headedness, she sat again. "I can't go. I can't do this."

"Just come for a visit. Meet everyone. See New Orleans."

"I can't, Nolan."

He took her hand again. Rubbed the top of it with his thumb. "Can we talk about it?"

She shook her head, crying in earnest now.

"Can you tell me why not?"

"Money." As soon as she said the word, more came rolling out, one on top of the other, like an avalanche. "It makes people crazy, Nolan. Makes them forget what really matters." The memories assailed her then and she was powerless to ignore them. They took her back over a decade ago. "The weather had been so bad that day," she told him, reliving the moment her life changed so drastically. "So bad. The sky was almost black, the kind where you get scared and just want to stay inside with the curtains closed and all the lights on. But when Barbara Mahoney called to say that the trip was still on, that the plane could go up, my parents didn't even think twice. They'd been planning the ski trip for weeks. Some famous actor was going to be there. Anyone who was anyone was going to be there. I'd heard my Mom talking about it on the phone to Aunt Betty. I begged them not to go. Begged them. I held on to my mom's arm, crying, trying to get her not to walk out that door, but she went, anyway. Because she was so driven by the temptation of being rich, she couldn't see the danger. Or she didn't see how the lure of money was changing her. She went right out that door and never came back…"

Nolan had suspected he'd been in love with Lizzie the year before. He'd been certain of it since his initial return to Austin.

Sitting on that couch with her on Christmas Eve, holding her while she shed what he guessed was over a decade of grief, he knew that the love was real. His throat grew tight and he cried a little bit, too, as he lived through the pain with her, felt her anguish.

A young girl, with no brothers and sisters, left an orphan, and she blamed wealth.

"Can I tell you something?" he asked several minutes after her sobs had died off. She'd been lying against him, her head on his shoulder, picking at a string on the back label of his tie.

"Real wealth has nothing to do with money." He was winging this one, speaking as it came to him. And yet, he'd never been more certain of anything. "My father... he could have forced a paternity test and tapped into his father's wealth, but he didn't want to be associated with someone who'd turn his back on the mother of his child, on his own child. So instead, he took the name, and made his own kind of wealth."

Her hand stilled on his chest.

"He had his father's acumen for numbers, his gift for making money, but he wasn't like him. My father's true wealth was in that dining room tonight. My mother— she sits right beside him so they can touch and talk— along the rest of us. Growing up, it wasn't my dad's money that made my life great—though I'm not going to kid you, I enjoy what I can buy. But all of my memories as a kid...they revolve around my brothers and sisters."

He sat her up, held her shoulders, looking her straight in the eye. "That's what I have to share with you in New Orleans, Lizzie. Brothers and sisters. Parents. A real family. They're a pain in the ass a lot of the time. And they run around and box up crazy stuff and wrap gifts.

"And Austin...giving you those old pants, it was his way of saying he trusts you with the family fortune. The intimate at-home stuff. Which, for him, is about as huge as it gets. He also said that if you don't bring it back—meaning, you don't come home with me—I lose my corner office with the windows. He wanted it, but I'd called it first."

"Can he do that?"

"No. But he can probably make my life a little more hellish at work if he really wanted to. Volunteer me to entertain the difficult clients."

When she smiled, his world flipped. He smiled back at her. And for a moment, it was a miracle.

"I don't like a lot of attention," she said, growing serious again. "I'm not the type of woman who is into wearing fancy clothes, and I've never gone to big society events. You move in a different world, Nolan, and I wouldn't want any of that to reflect badly on you and—"

"I am the one who screwed up," he interrupted. "I brought a child into the world, left her mother completely alone to deal with a life-threatening complication, all because I was too weak to face the challenge of falling in love."

Her expression changed again, a light shining in her eyes he hadn't seen in a year. "You fell in love?"

"Yeah," he said. "Didn't you?"

"Yes."

"So...we love each other."

"Yes."

"Then that means you should come to New Orleans with me and meet the rest of my family."

Her hesitation worried him, but not unduly so. He understood now why she hated money so acutely. And he looked forward to showing her the good sides to being financially blessed. She'd worked so hard to be all right and make something of her life—and even harder to provide security and love and happiness to their daughter. Now it was time for her to be taken care of.

"They have modest-size homes in New Orleans, too,"

he told her. He thought of the home in Austin he'd offered on. He was going to lose his thousand dollars on that one—forfeit it to the owners for backing out of the deal. But he didn't care one bit.

"I thought you had a fancy condo there."

"I do, and rooms at my folks' house, too. But I want you to choose your house. Be comfortable in it. And, you know, there are those Forte weekends. I've been doing them for years…and now we both can shed the wealth and just be…well, whatever we want to be."

"Oh, Nolan…"

"Just say you'll come. No, wait. I have an idea…"

He pulled out his phone, dialed and pushed to bring up a video call.

"Hey!"

"Bro!"

"Nolan!"

He made out the first three greetings; the rest were a mash of hellos.

"You there with her, son?" That was his father.

"Let me see her." His mother's face showed up on the screen. And Nolan moved over to put his face against Lizzie's.

"This is Lizzie, everyone. I made her cry."

She might hate him for the call, but his family was his best shot. They were the best part of him. And they always helped each other out of jams. That's what families were for.

A chorus of hellos followed as the screen filled with bunched-together faces. And then his mother was there again.

"Hi, Lizzie. I'm Sarah, but you can call me Mom, or whatever you'd like. You'll join us for lunch tomorrow, won't you? I can't wait to meet you. And to hold my very first grandchild." Sarah teared up then. "I can't believe I've missed the first three months of her life, and you… We'd have been there with you during the hard times, you know…"

"Give that to me." Miles's face filled the screen and then they could only see the back of his head as he turned to look at the rest of them. "Don't overwhelm her or Nolan will have to fight this one on his own," he warned. Then he turned back. "Welcome to our family, young lady. I hope to God you'll marry my son, but even if you don't, you're family now."

"Thank you," Lizzie said, sounding…good. Better than good. For Miles she found her voice. Didn't surprise Nolan at all. His dad was one special guy.

"So…you going to marry him?"

As she looked at Nolan, he pulled one more box out of his pocket. "This was the present my mom and dad sent me with," he said, holding the phone with one hand, while giving her the small box with the other. "It belonged to my Grandma Melton's mom and was to go to the mother of the first Fortune grandchild. And I thought maybe… Elizabeth Sullivan, will you marry me?"

Opening the box, she stared at the string of diamonds on the ring. It was more band than engagement ring, but he had a feeling Lizzie wouldn't want it any other way.

"Yes," she said, crying again, but her sniffles couldn't be heard over the whoops and hollers coming from his phone.

And from the hallway of the apartment, too.

In pj's and with a sleeping baby in her arms, Carmela stood there, tears streaming down her face.

Handing Lizzie the phone, Nolan walked over to her, took Stella and then led Carmela back to the living room with him, waiting until she sat down before he moved back to the phone. He owed her everything—having been there for his family when he was not. She was family now, too, and he'd do whatever he could to ease her way.

"Hey, everyone, meet the newest Fortune!" He scooted right up to Lizzie, placed Stella carefully half on him and half on her and turned the phone so his family could watch her sleep.

In the midst of softly spoken oohs and ahhs and even something about Stella having someone's nose, he could see what they saw, in the corner of his screen. A thumbnail of him and Lizzie and their daughter—Stella sleeping peacefully, secure, healthy and happy. And Lizzie, grinning like he'd never seen her grin before. She was happy, too. You could see it in her eyes. Truly happy. Maybe happier than she'd ever been.

His family, on-screen with his family.

It was a picture he was never going to forget.

* * * * *

The Fortunes of Texas will return next month in the new Special Edition continuity

The Fortunes of Texas:
The Lost Fortunes

Don't miss
A Deal Made in Texas *by Michelle Major*

On sale January 2019, wherever
Harlequin books are sold.

COMING NEXT MONTH FROM

H HARLEQUIN®

SPECIAL EDITION

Available December 18, 2018

#2665 A DEAL MADE IN TEXAS
The Fortunes of Texas: The Lost Fortunes • by Michelle Major
It's like a scene from Christine Briscoe dreams when the flirtatious attorney asks her to be his (pretend) girlfriend. But there is nothing make-believe about the sparks between the quiet office manager and the sexy Fortune scion. Are they heading for heartbreak...or down the aisle?

#2666 THE COWBOY'S LESSON IN LOVE
Forever, Texas • by Marie Ferrarella
Ever since Clint Washburn's wife left, he's built up defenses to keep everyone in Forever out—including his son. Now the boy's teacher, Wynona Chee, is questioning his parenting! And Clint is experiencing feelings he thought long dead. Wynona has her homework cut out for her if she's going to teach this cowboy to love again.

#2667 A NEW LEASH ON LOVE
Furever Yours • by Melissa Senate
Army vet Matt Fielding is back home, figuring out his new normal. Goal one: find his niece the perfect puppy. He never expected to find the girl he'd left behind volunteering at the local shelter. Matt can't refuse Claire's offer of puppy training but will he be able to keep his emotional distance this time around?

#2668 THE LAWMAN'S CONVENIENT FAMILY
Rocking Chair Rodeo • by Judy Duarte
When Adam Santiago teams up with music therapist Julie Chapman to save two young orphans, pretty soon *his* heart's a goner, too! Julie's willing to do anything—even become Adam's pretend bride—to keep a brother and sister together. Will this marriage of convenience become an affair of the heart?

#2669 TWINS FOR THE SOLDIER
American Heroes • by Rochelle Alers
Army ranger Lee Remington didn't think he'd ever go back to Wickham Falls, home of some of his worst memories. But he's shocked by a powerful attraction to military widow Angela Mitchell. But as he preps for his ready-made family, there's one thing Lee forgot to tell her...

#2670 WINNING CHARLOTTE BACK
Sweet Briar Sweethearts • by Kathy Douglass
Dr. Rick Tyler just moved in next door to Charlotte Shields. She thought she'd seen the last of him when he abandoned her at the altar but he's determined to make the move work for his young son. Will he get a second chance with Charlotte in the bargain?

HSECNM1218

Get 4 FREE REWARDS!

We'll send you 2 FREE Books plus 2 FREE Mystery Gifts.

Harlequin® Special Edition books feature heroines finding the balance between their work life and personal life on the way to finding true love.

FREE
Value Over
$20

"Lisa," the man dressed as Zorro said, "I'd heard you were
going to be here."

He clearly thought Julie was someone else. She probably
ought to say something, but up close, the gorgeous bandito
seemed to have stolen both her thoughts and her words.

"It's nice to finally meet you." His deep voice set her senses
reeling. "I've never really liked blind dates."

Talk about masquerades and mistaken identities. Before
Julie could set him straight, he took her hand in a polished,
gentlemanly manner and kissed it. His warm breath lingered on
her skin, setting off a bevy of butterflies in her tummy.

"Dance with me," he said.

Her lips parted, but for the life of her, she still couldn't
speak, couldn't explain. And she darn sure couldn't object.

Zorro led her away from the buffet tables and to the dance
floor. When he opened his arms, she again had the opportunity
to tell him who she really was. But instead, she stepped into his
embrace, allowing him to take the lead.

His alluring aftershave, something manly, taunted her. As
she savored his scent, as well as the warmth of his muscular
arms, her pulse soared. She leaned her head on his shoulder

as they swayed to a sensual beat, their movements in perfect accord, as though they'd danced together a hundred times before.

Now would be a good time to tell him she wasn't Lisa, but she seemed to have fallen under a spell that grew stronger with every beat of the music. The moment turned surreal, like she'd stepped into a fairy tale with a handsome rogue.

Once again, she pondered revealing his mistake and telling him her name, but there'd be time enough to do that after the song ended. Then she'd return to the kitchen, slipping off like Cinderella. But instead of a glass slipper, she'd leave behind her momentary enchantment.

But several beats later, a cowboy tapped Zorro on the shoulder. "I need you to come outside."

Zorro looked at him and frowned. "Can't you see I'm busy?"

The cowboy, whose outfit was so authentic he seemed to be the real deal, rolled his eyes.

Julie wished she could have worn her street clothes. Would now be a good time to admit that she wasn't an actual attendee but here to work at the gala?

"What's up?" Zorro asked.

The cowboy folded his arms across his chest and shifted his weight to one hip. "Someone just broke into my pickup."

Zorro's gaze returned to Julie. "I'm sorry, Lisa. I'm going to have to morph into cop mode."

Now it was Julie's turn to tense. He was actually a police officer in real life? A slight uneasiness settled over her, an old habit she apparently hadn't outgrown. Not that she had any real reason to fear anyone in law enforcement nowadays.

Don't miss
The Lawman's Convenient Family *by Judy Duarte,*
available January 2019 wherever
Harlequin® Special Edition books and ebooks are sold.

www.Harlequin.com

#1 *New York Times* bestselling author

LINDA LAEL MILLER

presents:

The next great contemporary read from
Harlequin Special Edition author Judy Duarte!
A touching story about the magic of creating a
family and developing romantic relationships.

*"Will you marry me, for a
while?"*

Adam Santiago's always
been a lone ranger. But
when the detective teams
up with music therapist
Julie Chapman to save
two young orphans, pretty
soon *his* heart's a goner,
too! Julie's willing to do
anything—even become
Adam's pretend bride—to
keep a brother and sister
together. But as she falls
head over heels for her polar opposite, will this marriage
of convenience become an affair of the heart?

**Available December 18,
wherever books are sold.**